FIGHTING MAN

OTHER FIVE STAR WESTERNS BY WAYNE D. OVERHOLSER:

FIGHTING MAN

A WESTERN DUO

WAYNE D. OVERHOLSER

FIVE STAR
A part of Gale, Cengage Learning

GALE
CENGAGE Learning

Detroit • New York • San Francisco • New Haven, Conn • Waterville, Maine • London

GALE
CENGAGE Learning®

LIBRARY OF CONGRESS CATALOGING-IN-PUBLICATION DATA

Overholser, Wayne D., 1906–1996.
  [Hate in his holster]
  Fighting man : a western duo / by Wayne D. Overholser. — 1st ed.
    p. cm.
    ISBN-13: 978-1-4328-2556-0(hardcover)
    ISBN-10: 1-4328-2556-9(hardcover)
  I. Title.
  PS3529.V33F55 2012
  813'.54—dc23   2011034864

First Edition. First Printing: January 2012.
Published in 2012 in conjunction with Golden West Literary Agency.

Printed in the United States of America
1 2 3 4 5 6 7 16 15 14 13 12

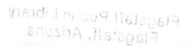

ADDITIONAL COPYRIGHT INFORMATION

"Hate in His Holster" by Wayne D. Overholser first appeared in *Western Novels and Short Stories* (4/49). Copyright © 1949 by Newsstand Publications, Inc. Copyright © renewed 1977 by Wayne D. Overholser. Copyright © 2012 by the Estate of Wayne D. Overholser for restored material.

"Fighting Man" by Wayne D. Overholser first appeared in *Best Western* (11/52). Copyright © 1952 by Stadium Publishing Corporation. Copyright © renewed 1980 by Wayne D. Overholser. Copyright © 2012 by the Estate of Wayne D. Overholser for restored material.

CONTENTS

★ ★ ★ ★ ★

HATE IN HIS HOLSTER

★ ★ ★ ★ ★

I

Dave Lanning was hitching the blacks to the spring wagon when old Bert Haney, the YT foreman, hobbled out of the ranch house and came over to the barn. Haney had ramrodded the YT as long as there had been a YT, and in his day had been as good a cowman as ever rode out of Texas, but weather, bad horses, and a rustler's bullet in his right leg had just about done him in. For more than a year Haney hadn't been on a horse, so it had fallen to Dave to do his running for him.

"Where you going?" Haney asked.

"Taking a load of salt to Buffalo Spring."

Haney pulled at his droopy mustache and moved on to lean against the corral. "Reckon I can take care of that chore. I ain't been to the spring for quite a spell."

"I guess you can get it there all right," Dave said, giving the old man a direct look.

He knew Haney like the palm of his hand, for Haney had brought him up from Texas with the herd years ago. The old man had been the only father he could remember. He had been five when the Comanches had made an orphan out of him; he'd existed for another five years in a tough trailside town, fighting for a living like a stray mongrel pup. Then Bert Haney had picked him up and brought him to western Nebraska, and from that day to this he had been part of the YT the same as old Bert had.

Watching Haney's effort to be casual, Dave knew that

11

something was wrong. It wasn't the old man's way to beat around the bush. He had loaded Dave with as much responsibility as a kid could take right from the first, saying that, if Dave's blood was good, he'd make a man out of him, and, if it wasn't, he'd break him and be done with it. Now, at twenty-three, Dave was older than his years in both looks and actions, and everybody on the upper Frenchman allowed that young Lanning was a man to ride the river with if you were on his side, and a man to duck if you weren't.

Haney got out his pipe and filled it. "I sure ain't much good no more," he grunted, "but if I don't do something now and then besides just sitting and hating the danged nesters, I'll go batty. Anyhow, I've got a chore for you." Haney handed an envelope to Dave. "Had a letter from the new owner yesterday."

Dave pulled out the single sheet, unfolded it, and read:

I expect to be in Sunfisher August 1st. Will you please see that there is a rig waiting at the depot to take me to the ranch.

Yours truly,
T. Benson

"So you want me to go meet this T. Benson?" Dave said. "Why didn't you come out and say so?"

"I was afraid maybe you wouldn't want to." Haney scratched a match on the top corral bar and lighted his pipe. "This here Benson has been danged ornery ever since he got the outfit, hollerin' about this and that because we ain't makin' enough. I didn't tell you about the letter I got last month." He took the pipe out of his mouth and spit into the dust. "Made me so mad I didn't sleep for a week. I wrote about buying them Winchesters and a hundred boxes of shells, and Benson curried me down for it. Wanted to know why we didn't quit hunting and go to work."

Dave laughed, not that it was really funny. It's never funny when nesters move in like a plague of grasshoppers and you don't know whether you're going to have any range at all or just a lot of sand for the wind to blow. Or maybe it was a little funny, this T. Benson wanting to know why they didn't go to work when they were all working their heads off, the YT running short-handed like it was because Benson kept saying that they had to cut expenses. What did some smart-aleck greenhorn back in St. Louis know about the cattle business?

"Maybe we ought to go to work," Dave said. "Go to work on Justin Tucker and a couple of hundred sodbusters he brought in here."

"Yeah," Haney muttered. "Maybe it's a good thing this Benson is coming out to look things over. We'll let him decide what to do with Tucker and the rest of 'em."

Dave glanced at the note again. The handwriting was legible, big letters almost perfectly formed. Dave had never seen writing like it before. He said: "Benson must not have anything to do but practice his writing."

"Practice writing his name on the back of our checks," Haney snorted. "Well, reckon you better put this team on the buggy and I'll take the bays. They don't move along like the blacks. I figger the less we do to gravel Benson the better."

"Sure, Bert."

While Dave unhitched the blacks and hooked them up to the buggy, he kept his eyes on Haney. The old man was mighty near sick. He hadn't been eating much lately. He kept laying it on his stomach, but Dave knew better. It was nothing but worry. He'd been worrying ever since old Bill Jockin died and this T. Benson had fallen heir to the YT. Jockin had been a straight shooter. He had visited the ranch once a year, knew all of Haney's troubles, and never made a kick if there wasn't a profit at the end of the year.

Haney had started worrying when Bill Jockin died. He'd never said so, but Dave knew he was afraid of losing his job. It was that fear that was working on him now. Apparently he'd never given it a thought when Jockin was alive, but not many owners were as understanding as old Bill. Besides, he had liked Haney personally. But this T. Benson didn't know Haney and he didn't know that the YT wouldn't even be in existence if it weren't for Bert Haney. If he fired Haney . . . ! Dave's lips tightened. The old man would die and T. Benson would be a killer the same as if he'd put a gun to Haney's head and pulled the trigger.

"We've got company!" Haney called.

Dave hooked up the last tug and turned to look. Three riders were coming. Dave couldn't be sure, but the big man in the middle looked like Justin Tucker.

"I was a mite worried about sending you to town," Haney said, "thinking you'd get into a ruckus with Tucker and that Sneed varmint, but I guess I can do my worrying at home. That's Tucker in the middle, ain't it?"

There was nothing wrong with Bert Haney's eyes. Dave waited a moment before he said: "Yeah, that's Tucker. His girl's with him. I don't know the fellow on the right."

"He don't want trouble or he'd have left his girl home," Haney muttered.

Dave lifted his gun from leather and checked it. "I wouldn't be sure, Bert. Tucker's a queer gent." He slipped the .45 back into the holster. "Better get your iron."

"No. If I don't have it, I won't use it."

They waited, Dave beside the buggy, Haney at the corral, until the three riders reined up. Justin Tucker was a big man, square-headed with iron-gray hair and a wide, jutting chin. He had been a judge back in Iowa, or so he claimed. Dave believed him, for he didn't look like a farmer, but he seemed to be a leader and the settlers had accepted him.

Dave had seen the girl in Sunfisher. Her name was Nona. A pretty name, he thought, and she was a pretty girl, small and shapely with blue eyes and curly black hair that always contrived to look wild and unruly. Now, as she reined up, she smiled at Dave, and he took off his Stetson, his heart pumping so hard that he found it difficult to breathe. He knew his face was red and he mentally termed himself a fool for acting like a kid, but Nona Tucker was the kind of girl who would set a fire under any man's heart.

The third rider was a man about thirty-five, a stranger to Dave. He looked like a cattleman in his wide-brimmed Stetson, spike-heeled boots, and flannel shirt with a bandanna around his neck, but he carried a thonged-down gun low on his right hip. Dave, giving him a straight look, decided he was a gunslick posing as a cowman.

"Good morning, Haney," Tucker said in a booming voice that befitted a judge. "This is my daughter Nona, and this"—he motioned to the other man—"is Rolf Jaeger."

"Howdy," Haney said civilly, and waited.

The girl smiled and Jaeger nodded coolly. His right hand, Dave noted, was never far from his gun butt, and anger began growing in Dave Lanning. If Tucker wanted trouble, he had no business bringing the girl, and, if he didn't want trouble, he had no business bringing Jaeger.

Tucker nodded at Dave. He said: "How are you, Lanning?" He made no effort to mention either his daughter or Jaeger again.

The anger that had been simmering in Dave began to boil. He looked at Nona Tucker, his Stetson still in his hand. "Ma'am, I'm Dave Lanning. I've seen you in town several times, but reckon you didn't know me."

Tucker chewed a meaty lip, his cheeks getting red. "She

wouldn't have any reason to know you, Lanning."

"Maybe not, but she does now."

Nona smiled again, her teeth white and perfect between red lips. "You're wrong, Father. I have seen Mister Lanning in town. He's a man you couldn't help noticing."

Dave put his hat on, meeting the girl's eyes squarely. "Ma'am, you're as purty as a new red-wheeled buggy, but it sure puzzles me how you happened to draw a land pirate for a father and why you're riding with a gunslick like Jaeger."

Nona sobered. "Thank you for the compliment, Mister Lanning."

Tucker's face froze. "You're mistaken about who's a land pirate, Lanning. It's YT that's claiming the country south of the Frenchman."

It was Rolf Jaeger who understood Dave. The small grin that curled the corners of his thin-lipped mouth was faintly mocking. "A mite proddy, ain't you, Lanning?"

"Yeah. Proddy as hell . . . excuse me, ma'am. What are your intentions, Jaeger?"

"No sense pushing this hairpin, Dave," Haney cut in. "We'll listen to what they've got to say and then they'll slope out of here."

"That's right," Jaeger murmured. "You've got me wrong, Lanning. I'm no gunslick. I own Skull, a fair-sized outfit east of here."

"Then how come you're traveling with nesters?" Dave demanded.

"I ain't exactly traveling with 'em," Jaeger said. "I just took the ride out here for the charming company." He motioned toward Nona. "You don't blame me, do you?"

"No, but maybe it's more'n the company. Maybe you've got your own irons in the fire."

"Yes, I have one iron. It's the old story, Lanning, settlers plowing the grass under in my country, so I'm moving west. I've got to find a place to stop. Maybe here. Or in Colorado. Got any ideas, Lanning?"

"I've got one damned good one, Jaeger . . . excuse me, ma'am. Keep riding. We've got enough trouble with Tucker's grangers without fighting another cow outfit."

"Now I suppose you have," Jaeger said, his voice deceptively mild, "but I think I'll look around some before I take your advice."

"Haney, why is Lanning talking for you?" Justin Tucker pinned his dark eyes on the foreman. "I came here to see you, not a tough cowhand."

"I'm old and worn out," Haney said in a sour, biting voice. "It's up to Dave to save YT from your fool sodbusters, if it is to be saved. If I hadn't had him for a *segundo,* we'd have been finished afore now."

"Very well," Tucker said coldly. "I'll tell you what we came for. You have set the Frenchman up as the north boundary of your range. You've made that stick because this county has been run by stockmen. That day is gone, Haney. Another wagon train pulled in yesterday. That will give us a majority at the polls as soon as these men have established their voting rights. Without the support of the county officials, you will have to grant the homesteaders their rights south of the river."

Haney began filling his pipe, shoulders bent, an old man as useless as a worn tool. "Perhaps, Tucker, but was I you, I wouldn't advise your people to cross the Frenchman today."

"Unless they want to fight," Dave added.

"I had hoped you would see the inevitability of your defeat," Tucker said bitterly. He swung his horse. Jaeger nodded amiably and reined around to follow Tucker, but Nona made no effort to leave. Good humor was back in her and Dave could not mistake the invitation that her eyes gave him.

17

Dave did not think. It was quick pulse that made him ask: "Can I take you to the dance Saturday night, ma'am?"

Justin Tucker swung around in the saddle, bawling: "No, Lanning. Your advances. . . ."

"You're an old fuddy-duddy, Father," Nona cut in. "We may be on opposite sides, but that is no reason why we can't be friends. I'll expect you, Mister Lanning."

For a moment Tucker's face was black with fury. He said: "Don't think my daughter is an avenue by which you can gain concessions from me. The settlers will have their rights if it means the finish of your YT."

Tucker rode off then, the square angle of his shoulders showing the defiance that lingered in him. Jaeger laughed softly and followed Tucker, but Nona hesitated as if not wanting to leave while this spirit of anger was upon them. She said: "Even my father makes mistakes. I never apologize for them." She nodded, lips still holding her friendly smile. Then she swung her horse and caught up with Tucker and Jaeger.

Haney stared after them, leathery face held rigid. "It ain't right, Dave. I don't know where it's off, but I know danged well it ain't right."

"The smell's bad for a fact." Dave stepped into the buggy seat. "Better have Luke cook up something special for supper."

"I'll tell him," Haney said. "And you stay out of trouble with Kip Sneed."

II

It was not yet noon when Dave reached Sunfisher. It was still a tiny trail-straddling town, the railroad having reached it only the spring before. Half a dozen frame buildings reared false fronts along the dusty street and soddies were scattered haphazardly at both ends of the business block. It was a hot day with a hot wind that squealed against the eaves and whipped dust down the street in a choking fog, at times hiding the circle of covered wagons east of town. It would be, Dave thought, the settlers' train that Tucker had mentioned.

Dave racked the team, seeing the Tuckers' and Rolf Jaeger's horses in front of the hotel. He stepped into the lobby to get out of the dust, wondering what T. Benson would think of western Nebraska. He wondered, too, and it was a senseless question that had plagued him for months, what the T. stood for? Ted. Timothy. Thaddeus. There were fifty names that ran through his mind, and the upshot of the whole thing was his conviction that he wouldn't like Benson. Anybody but a crank would sign his first name.

The clerk said: "Howdy, Dave. What's new on YT?"

"Not much. Sneed been up to any of his tricks?"

"It's the same trick. Still looking for beef at his price," the clerk scowled. "He says he'll have plenty when the settlers get started. They've all got a few cows and they'll need cash money so bad they'll sell at his figure."

"Maybe, if you can call their critters beef."

Dave walked on into the dining room and ordered a steak. The blonde Swedish waitress moved to the kitchen in stately grace, and Dave, leaning back in his chair, stretched his long legs under the table. If it wasn't for Bert Haney, he would saddle up and ride on. He wasn't sure where. He would just keep going until he saw mountains with trees on them. He was mighty tired of looking at nothing but buffalo grass and rolling sand hills.

He straightened up and built a smoke. He knew, when he made himself stop and think about it, that it wasn't the country that was sandpapering his temper. Actually it was fighting nesters and the weather and selfish businessmen like this Kip Sneed, all the time trying to hold a ranch together for a gent like this T. Benson. The truth was he didn't give a damn about Benson. He should be starting his own outfit. The time for a man to begin working for himself was when he was young. But he knew that as long as Bert Haney was alive and ramrodding YT, he'd ride along with him.

He had his steak and was reaching for the ketchup when the Tuckers came in with Rolf Jaeger. Justin Tucker gave him a cold stare, Jaeger nodded affably, and Nona's smile was like a ray of sunshine breaking through a bank of storm clouds. They moved across the room to a table set against the wall. They were too far away for Dave to hear their talk, but he saw that Jaeger was arguing for something and Tucker kept shaking his head. Then Nona said in a loud voice that reached Dave: "We're not rustlers. Don't try to make thieves and killers out of us."

Jaeger half rose from his chair, eyes swiveling to Dave, but Dave kept on eating as if he hadn't heard. Jaeger dropped back and said something in a low voice to Nona that brought an angry return from Tucker. Then Jaeger regained control of himself and was apologizing, donning again his usual affable manner.

Finishing, Dave paid for his meal and went back into the lobby. It was still half an hour before train time, so he loitered beside the desk, talking to the clerk.

When there was a lull in the conversation, Dave asked: "Who is this Rolf Jaeger?"

"Dunno, but he's sure thick with Sneed and Tucker." The clerk shook his head gloomily. "Don't mean nothing maybe, but I don't like the way things are shaping up. A few tough nesters, like young Charlie Morgan, are talking about chasing cows and riders into Colorado so they can claim land south of the Frenchman without no trouble."

"Sounds like some of that sneaking Sneed's work," Dave said.

"I don't like them names!" a man called.

Dave wheeled. Kip Sneed stood in the doorway, red, muscle-ridged face showing the pressure of his anger. Trouble between him and the YT had gone back almost to the day Bert Haney had brought Bill Jockin's herd up from Texas. He was a butcher who had made his pile selling beef to railroad construction camps, and he'd had the idea he could get cheap YT beef, but Haney had refused to sell. Now, for no reason that Dave knew, Sneed had settled in Sunfisher and opened a butcher shop, but he still refused to pay the market price for beef.

"Now maybe you don't like the names," Dave said coolly, "but they sure as the devil fit."

Sneed's ham-like hands fisted. "I've been wanting to do this for a long time, Lanning. Come out here."

"Go get a gun," Dave said.

"I'm not a gunman," Sneed snarled, "but I'll bust you up if you ain't too yellow to come out here."

Sneed was a bigger man than Dave and he had earned an evil reputation in the towns along the U.P. as a dirty fighter. Dave would have refused if he hadn't seen the Tuckers come out of the dining room and heard Rolf Jaeger say: "Funny about tough talkers. When it gets down to cases, they're nothing but wind."

Unbuckling his gun belt, Dave handed it to the clerk. He said: "All right, Sneed."

Nona Tucker cried out: "No . . . !"

Her father silenced her with a quick gesture. He said: "Sneed's doing our fighting."

Kip Sneed backed into the street, great shoulders hunched forward, beady black eyes bright with anticipation. He waited until Dave stepped off the boardwalk, then drove at him, huge fists clubbing at Dave's face.

As a boy Dave had learned to take care of himself, an art he'd continued to develop after Haney had brought him north, but he had never fought a man like Kip Sneed. The butcher was fast for one of his size; he was strong and without scruples. There was only one way to beat him, and that was to stay out of his reach until some of his great strength had been drained out of him.

Dave turned his head, Sneed's right fist ruffling his hair, and twisted aside as Sneed's left hammered at him. Then, with Sneed off balance, he caught him on the jaw with a short, driving right. Sneed went off his feet, head cracking against the end of a water trough.

From the hotel porch Nona Tucker cried out in sheer joy: "Hit him again, Dave!"

A crowd had gathered, most of them nesters, and their cheers were for Sneed. That was to be expected, for these men knew Dave as YT's fighting man, and it had been his job to deliver the ultimatum to stay north of the Frenchman, but the thing Dave didn't understand was Nona's support.

Dave had no time to consider such intangibles as a woman's feelings. Sneed came up to his hands and knees, shook his great head, and lunged at Dave like a freight train going down a mountain grade without brakes. He looked that big to Dave.

It was duck and feint, pivot and lash out with stinging fists. Keep out of the big man's deadly grip and give as much punishment as he could. Play it out until his chance came. Roll his shoulders, or use his elbows to save his face and body. Keep a fist in Sneed's face, quick, rapier-like blows that closed an eye, opened an old cut on his cheek, flattened his nose, and brought a rush of blood.

They were yelling at Dave to stand and fight, but the sound was a distant wordless flow of sound that meant nothing to him. He fought a cool-headed fight, holding himself to his plan, but when there was a moment of respite, he glimpsed Nona Tucker at the edge of the boardwalk, shouting for him and swinging her fists belligerently and jumping around like a Sioux at a war dance, the anxiety in her face proving the sincerity of her support.

Dave was never sure how it happened. Maybe he'd turned his eyes once too often to Nona. It seemed to come out of nowhere, Kip Sneed's big fist that caught him on the head like the swinging blow of an axe handle. Dave went down into the deep dust and rolled over. He wasn't out but for a moment the sun was a blinding blur of light. He sensed rather than saw Sneed lumbering toward him to smash his ribs with his wide-toed boots, and rolled again.

The racket of the crowd beat at Dave like ominous growling of thunder. Through it came Nona's begging voice: "Get up, Dave. Get up. You've got to get up." Somehow Dave did get up. The street and the crowd and big Kip Sneed all melting into a distant scene completely vague in its details. He took a step and someone tripped him.

Nona was across the dust strip like a darting terrier, crying: "Give him a chance, you sneaking coyote!" She beat at the man with her fists and he ran. Surprised, Sneed paused to look, and that was his mistake, for Dave was on him, his vision cleared. He brought a right through to the butcher's big chin, and the man went down.

Dave stood over him, rubbing his knuckles while Sneed wiped the blood out of his one good eye and came back to his feet. A locomotive's whistle cut through the crowd's racket, and for the first time since the fight started Dave remembered T. Benson. Now he reversed himself and carried the fight to Sneed, taking chances he had not taken before.

He smelled and tasted his own blood; he felt the shock of each blow he landed travel up his arms. He kept Sneed backing up until he was against the hitch pole. Then Sneed fell forward and gripped him, a battered hulk fighting more by instinct than design. Dave wrestled with him, keeping him smothered. He heard again the shrill train whistle and he wondered if he could finish this in time.

Sneed was clinging to Dave, squeezing him, trying to knee him, trying to batter him with his head. Suddenly Dave swung aside and broke loose, cracking the butcher hard on the chin. Sneed, unsupported, fell on his face. He raised himself on his arms and stared at Dave, his one good eye bright with hate.

Dave said: "Get up."

Sneed tried and fell back. He said through battered lips: "The devil with you, I'm licked."

Dave swung to the horse trough and sloshed water over his face. His head ached and there was a bruise below his right eye. He picked up his Stetson and went into the hotel lobby for his gun. When he came out, his belt was buckled around him. The crowd was still there. Somebody was helping Sneed to his feet. Nona Tucker was gone, so was Rolf Jaeger, but Tucker was there and he was still angry. He seemed to be angry most of the time, Dave thought.

"You made a fool out of my daughter," Tucker said ominously. "I won't have you seeing her. I won't stand for it. Do you understand?"

"Yeah, I understand," Dave said. "I understand you're plain loco. And I aim to see Nona if she'll see me. If you don't like it, you know where you can go."

Tucker choked, his wide face scarlet with rage. "Don't try to see her, Lanning. I'm telling you. Don't try it."

The train was pulling into the station now, bell clanging, but Dave didn't move. He ignored Tucker, gaze sweeping the circle of men. He asked: "Who was the ornery son-of-a-bitch that tripped me?"

No one answered. They looked down, none meeting his eyes. Some began backing away. Tucker cried: "Don't let him intimidate you. There'll come a day when we'll have a town marshal in Sunfisher, and, when that day comes, there will be no more brawling in the street."

Without another word Dave turned to his team. When he drove around the block to the depot, the crowd had scattered. Smoke and steam made a fog back along the track. Mailbags had been thrown out. Valises were piled at the end of the depot. Dave tied his team, eyes searching the crowd. He didn't have the slightest idea what T. Benson looked like. He supposed the YT owner would be a young man, or maybe a middle-aged one, but not an old one, for Haney had said that Benson was some kind of a relative of Bill Jockin. A nephew, Haney had guessed. He'd probably be a dude in a hard hat, but no such man was in sight.

Dave walked along the train and swung back, a sourness washing through him. There wasn't anybody here who looked like he might be T. Benson. That meant he hadn't come, and Dave would have to wait for the midnight train. Then he was back at the buggy and he stopped, flat-footed, for a woman stood beside the rig, waiting impatiently for him. When he came up, she asked him with biting irony: "You wouldn't by the least chance be looking for someone, would you?"

Dave cuffed back his Stetson and rubbed his bruised face, temper worn thin. He had never seen the woman before. Evidently she'd come on the train, for she had none of the marks of the West upon her. She was young, probably in her early twenties, tall and slender and handsome, if you liked a positive, almost mannish kind of woman. Dave sensed the positive quality immediately. She wore a dark severely tailored suit and a wide-brimmed straw hat with a red bow; her chin was pointed and firm, and her hazel eyes had a way of taking a man's hide off like a pair of sharp-bladed knives.

"Yeah, I was looking for somebody." Dave stepped into the buggy. "He didn't come."

"Who would that be?" the woman demanded, not moving. "Somebody named T. Benson perhaps?"

Dave picked up the lines, staring at her while a terrible fear began working in him. "That's right. I'm looking for T. Benson."

"Then you're from the YT," the woman said icily. "Get out of there and put my valise back of the seat. I'm Thelma Benson."

III

Mechanically Dave obeyed, a sickness gripping the pit of his stomach. The woman watched him with cool indifference, her gaze sweeping down his lanky whip-muscled body, pausing briefly on the holstered gun, and returned to his bruised face.

"From the dirt on your clothes and the bruise on your cheek," she said in a chill voice, "I assume that you've been involved in a street brawl. Is that why you weren't here when the train got in?"

"Yes, ma'am. I'm Dave Lanning. You ought to see Kip Sneed. He's got more'n dust on his pants and a bruise on his cheek."

Her face flushed with anger. "I don't care what you did to this Kip Sneed. I wrote to Bert Haney that I'd be here today, but when the train stopped, no one was here. Where is Haney?"

Dave dragged a boot toe through the dust. "Well, now, you see, ma'am, he's taking some salt over to Buffalo Spring."

For an instant he thought she was going to explode in his face. Her lips trembled and her cheeks were redder than any sunset Dave had ever seen, but she held her anger under control. She asked: "I am led to believe, then, that Bert Haney considered it more important to haul salt to cattle than to meet me?"

Dave had figured he wouldn't like her the minute he'd seen her. Now he was sure he didn't. He said: "No, ma'am. He just sent me to do this chore. I'll take you over to the hotel now."

"Hotel? Look, Lanning, in case you're mixed up. I'm the T. Benson who owns the YT. I inherited it from my uncle, Bill Jockin."

"Yeah, I know. I said I'd take you to the hotel."

She stepped into the buggy. "You'll take me out to the ranch. What makes you think I want to go to a hotel?"

"Well, you see, ma'am, the YT ain't what you'd call a woman's ranch. Ain't never been no women there except once. Old Missus Parrot came out when Bert got sick and needed nursing. You wouldn't like it."

"I'll like it," she said crisply. "I'll have to. I told you I own it."

"Sure, but owning it and liking it are two different things. There just ain't no place for a woman to stay."

"There's beds, aren't there? And there's food to eat, isn't there? There's a house, isn't there?"

"If you call our bunks beds, we've got beds. Luke Farr, he's the cook, claims the stuff he puts on the table is grub, and, as for the house, we've got a soddy, but if it rains, you'll have mud running down your neck."

"I suppose you'd rather take me to a hotel." Her eyes were as frosty as a December morning. "Then put me on the next train that goes East."

"It'd be a right good idea, ma'am. The YT ain't no place for a woman. We'll wait till morning and I'll take you out there. You look things over and talk to Bert, and I'll bring you back to town."

She sat with her hands on her lap, fingers laced. "Lanning, I will not have a man on my payroll who can't or won't take orders. I haven't had my dinner. Take me to a restaurant. As soon as I eat, you'll take me to the YT. If you want to keep your job, you'll stop arguing,"

He had some things he wanted to say—like he didn't give a damn whether he kept his job or not and she could go jump

27

into the Frenchman as far as he was concerned—but he didn't say them. He'd wait for Bert to blow up. It was his guess that wouldn't take long.

Dave stepped into the buggy and sat down beside her. "Yes, ma'am," he said with deceptive mildness as he reached for the lines. He had not noticed Rolf Jaeger leaning against the depot until the man stepped forward and raised his Stetson in a gracious gesture.

"Excuse me, ma'am," Jaeger said, "but I assume that you're the YT owner?"

"That's right."

"I'm Rolf Jaeger. I want to welcome you to Sunfisher. My outfit is Skull. Up till now we've been east of here, but we're moving west, so we'll be neighbors."

"The devil we will," Dave said hotly. "Don't hand out none of that gab. We've got all the neighbors now we can stand."

"Shut up, Lanning," Thelma ordered. "I'm pleased to meet you, Mister Jaeger."

Jaeger stepped back toward the depot. "If there is anything I can do for you, Miss Benson, let me know. I shall be only too happy to oblige."

"Thank you, Mister Jaeger. All right, Lanning."

Dave held his tongue, but he was boiling. The surest way for YT to commit suicide was to invite Jaeger and his outfit into the YT's range, or just to be friendly to Jaeger and give him a chance to shoot the YT hands in the back. The trouble was Dave didn't really know anything about Jaeger, but he had a feeling they were all together, Sneed and Tucker and Jaeger, and they meant to bust YT. He tied the blacks in front of the hotel, knowing she wouldn't believe anything he told her even if he had proof that Jaeger was a crook.

"There's a dining room inside, ma'am," Dave said.

She got down and went in, not giving him a glance or the

trace of a smile. Dave moved to the shade of the hotel, built a smoke, and hunkered there, his dislike for Thelma Benson growing by the minute. Presently Jaeger came by, nodded, fingered the ash from his cigar, and went inside. Dave flipped his cigarette stub into the street and turned into the lobby. Looking into the dining room, he saw Justin Tucker and Jaeger were sitting at Thelma's table, Jaeger leaning forward and talking earnestly.

Dave swore softly and sat down in a corner chair. He built another cigarette and fired it, eyes moodily on the street. He didn't like any part of it. If T. Benson had been a man, as he had expected, he would have some idea how to deal with him, but when T. Benson turned out to be a woman, he was up a tree. He thought of delivering her to the ranch and riding on, and immediately knew he wouldn't do it any more than he had the last five hundred times he'd thought about it. Nothing was changed. The only thing that would make any real difference would be for Thelma to fire Haney, and that was too much to expect even from her.

Dave was still sitting there when Thelma came out of the dining room, Tucker on one side of her, Jaeger on the other. Dave rose, asking: "Ready to go, ma'am?"

"Yes," she said coldly, "but Mister Jaeger will take me. From what they tell me, I see that my judgment of you is right."

Temper, already raw, now drove him forward toward her. "What is that judgment?"

"That you're a brawler and a troublemaker. Mister Jaeger says it's twenty miles to YT. I'm afraid to ride that far with you."

He licked his lips. No woman had ever said that to him before. He looked at the faintly smiling Jaeger, to Tucker whose square face held an expression of triumph. He started toward the door, his natural feeling being that the lot of them could go hang. Then he stopped. Old ties of loyalty were not that easily broken. Everything that Bert Haney had built would be destroyed if this crazy woman was let have her head. Haney had to have his chance with her.

Dave swung back to Thelma: "You're a little mixed-up on who's your friend. You're going with me."

"Now, Lanning . . . ," Jaeger began.

Dave's gun was in his hand. "When I first saw you this morning, Jaeger, I had a notion that sooner or later you 'n' me would be swapping smoke, but I don't reckon it's quite time yet. Now just stay out of this."

Jaeger turned to Thelma, making a quick gesture as if to tell her there was nothing he could do. "You see how it is with him? He thinks first of his fists or a gun, but even out here there are many things that cannot be settled with either."

He was smooth, this Rolf Jaeger. Dave said: "Ma'am, you can walk to the buggy, or I'll pick you up and tote you out there, and I'll shoot Jaeger if he raises a hand."

"Maybe you'd better go," Jaeger said. "Not that I value my own life so much, but if I was killed now, there would be a great deal of trouble. After you're out there, you can iron things out."

"I don't think he'll hurt you, Miss Benson," Tucker conceded. "These cowboys have a deep respect for a woman."

"That's the first honest thing you've said since you showed up here, Tucker," Dave breathed.

Nona had come down the stairs. Dave did not know how much she had heard, but she walked across the lobby to stand beside Thelma, her head high. She said: "If there is any man to fear in this country, it's Rolf Jaeger."

"Now that isn't kind." Jaeger acted as if her words deeply injured him.

"Go back upstairs, Nona!" Tucker bawled. "You're mixing with things you don't understand."

30

"I understand more than you think I do, Father." Nona laid a hand on Thelma's arm. "If you want me to, I'll ride with you to the YT. Dave can bring me back in the morning, or lend me a horse."

For the first time doubt seemed to be in Thelma Benson. She looked helplessly at Nona, then at Justin Tucker. "This is your daughter?"

Tucker had almost lost control of himself. His lips were working; his dark eyes were the eyes of a wild man. "She's my daughter," he said savagely, "although there are times when I wonder whether I should claim her. For some reason, Miss Benson, she has taken a liking to this man, Lanning, and a dislike to Rolf Jaeger. She's young and youth is full of mistakes."

"I see." Thelma drew her arm away from Nona's hand. "You won't have to go, Miss Tucker."

Thelma turned toward the door. Tucker said with ill-subdued violence: "Nona, go to your room. You've butted into my business for the last time."

"Not the last," she flung at him, "unless I'm dead, or you give up this crazy thing that Jaeger has got you into."

"Thanks for your help in the fight, Nona," Dave said.

"You didn't need any help," she said quickly. "I enjoyed watching it. There's only one man I'd rather have seen licked than Kip Sneed."

For that moment their eyes met, and something happened to Dave Lanning, something that was new and wonderful and stirring. He said: "I'll see you Saturday night."

"Of course, Dave. Or maybe sooner."

Tucker laid a big hand on Nona's arm and pushed her toward the stairs. She jerked free, gave Dave a quick smile that was reflected in her blue eyes. Then she swung away and went up the stairs.

Dave pinned his gaze on Tucker's wide face. He said, his tone held ominously low: "I don't savvy some of this, but maybe Nona's trying to make an honest man out of a crook. I just want you to get one thing straight. If you harm her in any way, I'll kill you."

Jaeger, the small, faintly mocking smile on his lips, said: "For a brawler and a troublemaker, friend, you show a great regard for the girl."

"That's right. See that you do the same."

Dave swung out of the lobby and untied the team. Thelma was standing beside the buggy. She got into the seat now and Dave sat down beside her, saying: "One of these days you'll be sorry you said what you did about being afraid to ride with me."

"I'm not usually sorry for things I do or say, Lanning," she said coldly.

"You've made every mistake you could since you got here," he went on harshly, "but there's one you'd better not make. That's to hurt Bert."

"If I do?"

"I'll turn you across my lap and spank you like your ma should have done a long time ago."

He thought she'd slap him, but she didn't. Her smile cut some of the harshness from her face. She said mildly: "Lanning, I believe you would."

IV

They headed straight west from Sunfisher, the hot wind cutting at them and sprinkling them with gray dust. Thelma kept patting her skirt, trying to keep the dust out of it until she saw she could not and gave up. Her hat was pinned firmly to her reddish-blonde hair, but she clutched it with her left hand, the brim curled up against the red bow.

For an hour they rode in silence, the sun driving its hard rays directly at them. Thelma licked dry lips and lowered her head against the wind. Dave glanced at her, knowing that she was suffering and having no pity for her. She didn't have any business out here in the first place. If she couldn't trust Bert Haney's judgment, she didn't deserve a ranch.

She turned her head to look at him, bringing the hat brim down to shade her eyes. "Lanning, you said I'd made every mistake I could since I got here. What did you mean?"

"I mean you're a blamed stubborn woman," he said bluntly. "What do you know about the cattle business? Or about anything out here?"

"I know people," she answered. "I know what should be the relationship between employer and hired hands. I see that's something you don't know."

"Maybe not, but I still know more about it than you do. If you keep up the way you've started, you won't even have an outfit in a week."

He stared straight ahead, feeling her eyes on him. They were on a bench above the river, the meandering Frenchman to their left. There was a flat on the other side of the stream, and on to the south the sand hills made long rolls on the face of the prairie. They swung toward the river, crossed it, and kept upstream, but, if Thelma Benson was aware of the country around her, she gave no indication of it. She kept her eyes on Dave's long bronzed face for a time, then brought her gaze away and lowered her head.

"I realize that conditions are different in this kind of a country," she said, the wind whipping her words away from Dave so that he had to bend toward her to hear them. "But I also know that there are certain business principles which should not be violated. Before Uncle Bill died, he showed me the figures on the YT, and he told me to trust this Bert Haney you seem so fond of."

"Then you'd better do it," Dave snapped.

"But in the year or more that I've owned the YT," she went on, "the income has been far below what it was when Uncle Bill owned it. Haney reports expenditures for this and that which seem useless."

"Like Winchesters and a hundred boxes of Thirty-Thirty shells?"

"That's right," she said defiantly.

He looked at her, his gray eyes scornful. "What do you want us to do, sit around with empty guns that are plumb worn out, or do you want us to fight for your outfit?"

"Fight? Why should there be any fighting?"

"Because the nesters are pushing us." He pointed to a man building a soddy on the other side of the river. "There's the whole story. Covered wagon, a man and his wife, and six kids. They hate us because we've told 'em not to cross the river. Maybe they can get a crop here, if they get rain, but on this side the dirt's no good for farming. Plow up the grass and the wind will move the whole damned country."

"Have you told them that?"

Dave laughed sourly. "We've told 'em, but they don't listen good. Not even Justin Tucker. They think we're lying because we want to keep 'em off our range, so Tucker goes on advertising in the papers back East about the free land out here, and they keep coming. They'll tear up the grass and maybe raise a crop or two, then they'll get some dry years and they're finished. So are we if we let 'em cross the river."

"They haven't crossed yet?"

"No, but they'll try. A new bunch just got in. Tucker and Jaeger were out this morning telling us they aim to run the county."

"Rolf Jaeger is a cowman. Why can't you co-operate?"

"Looks like a gunslick to me," Dave said, "maybe brought in by Tucker to knock a few of us off."

34

"He owns Skull."

"I think he's lying."

Again they drove in silence, Thelma sitting with her head lowered, hat brim pulled down over her forehead. She was thinking over what he had said, but whether he had convinced her of anything or not was a question in his mind.

Minutes later she said: "Tell me about Bert Haney."

He gave her the story, of how Bill Jockin had trusted Haney with a herd, of Haney's picking Dave up and bringing him on, of troubles with the Sioux and rustlers. Then he said: "The YT is Bert's. He made it. No matter who owns it, he made it. Funny about Bert. The YT's a part of him. He's loyal. Not to Bill Jockin or you. He's loyal to the YT. Our hands come and go, and I hang on 'cause of Bert. When he goes, there ain't no more YT. If you fired him, he'd go off and die. You understand?"

"No, I don't," she said quickly. "A cattle ranch is a business. There's no place for sentiment in it."

His lips tightened, jaw muscles standing out like small marbles. "You play it that way, ma'am, and you'll go broke. You can't run a cow outfit like a factory."

"I'll show you," she said hotly. "If we have to fight nesters, we'll fight them, and I'll pay as good wages as anybody but I expect every man to earn what I pay him."

He didn't say anything more. He couldn't. He understood now why Bert Haney hadn't been able to eat. The old man had sensed, perhaps from Thelma's letter, what was coming. She aimed to fire him as sure as purgatory was hot.

They wheeled into the ranch yard with the sun a red ball hanging above the western horizon. It was a wild breathless land, the sky and earth running out until they met, a land of empty miles waiting for a decision between the nesters and the cattlemen, an old fight, unchanging in suffering and terror and violence. The blasting guns would sound the same; death would be the same. The difference lay in the personalities of those who decided the issues, and in geography. Here, on the south side of the Frenchman, geography favored the cattlemen, but nesters were notorious for failing to observe the rules of geography until forced to do so.

Haney had seen the buggy when it was a long way off. He had been watching for it since noon. Now, as Dave drove into the yard, Haney stood beside the windmill, hands jammed into pockets, a bent-shouldered, gnarled old man.

Dave pulled up, looking at Thelma, and the sickness in him became a dull ache for he saw in her face what she aimed to do. He might have changed her notions about some things, but not on this business of sentiment.

"Bert, this is T. Benson," Dave said. "Miss Benson, this here is your foreman."

She extended a slim hand, and Haney took it in his rope-scarred one, his face mirroring astonishment. He held her hand a moment, faded eyes searching hers, and then he said: "Welcome, Miss Benson. I sure didn't figger on you being a woman."

"I have been a woman all my life, Mister Haney," she said. "I didn't tell you because some men are prejudiced about working for women."

"I reckon," Haney said heavily.

Stepping down, Dave gave Thelma a hand. "I'll fetch your valise as soon as I take care of the horses."

She nodded absently, her gaze swinging from the sod house to the windmill whirling above her and on to the frame barn and barbed-wire corrals. A hay meadow stretched northward toward the river, the stacks dark bulks in the field. This had been Dave's home for years, the only real home he could remember. As far as he was concerned, everything was the way it should be, but he saw that it was not to her liking. She bit her chapped lips, raised a hand to her wind-burned cheek, and said: "I'd like a drink of water, Haney."

When Dave came back, Haney and Thelma were standing in front of the house. He was talking to her about the place, pointing to something down the river, but he broke off when he heard Dave, and swung to face him.

"You have a scrap with Sneed?" Haney asked.

"We had a tussle." Dave gingerly felt of the bruise on his cheek. "I told him to get a gun, but he didn't cotton to the notion."

"How did you know it was with this Sneed, whoever he is?" Thelma asked Haney. "I didn't tell you and Lanning hasn't had a chance."

"Sneed's been kicking up a dust for a long time," Haney said. "We don't know what he's after, but he's been plumb thick with this nester bunch that's come in. It's my guess Sneed figgers, and he's sure right, that Dave's the one who's keeping the settlers north of the river. If he can run Dave out of the country, he's got us licked."

"You're the foreman, Haney."

"Well, in a way, ma'am, but I'm all stove up. Dave's the fighting man. You've got some good boys. Don't make no mistake about that, but they've got to have a leader. Dave's it."

"I see." Thelma laid speculative eyes on Dave. "I hadn't thought of you in quite that way, Lanning. Maybe that's the reason you find it hard to obey orders."

"Maybe," Dave said.

Haney looked at him sharply. "Now what's this?"

"I didn't want to bring her out till morning."

"We don't have no good accommodations for a lady, ma'am," Haney said heavily. "Now that's a fact."

"I'll get along." Thelma swung toward the house. "Bring the valise, Lanning."

She stopped just inside the door, her gaze swinging around the cluttered room. She took her time, staring at the rough board floor, the magnesia plastered walls, the poor furniture largely handmade from boxes. Turning, she asked: "There is an extra bedroom, isn't there, Lanning?"

"No, not what you'd call a bedroom, but we can fix a bed in the office." He jerked a thumb at a door to their left. "Bert's got an old leather couch in there."

"All right." Her voice was almost a groan. "Take my valise in, and bring me some water."

He carried the valise into the office. When he came back, he said sharply: "There's a bucket in back. You can tote your own water."

He swung out of the room, feeling the hot anger that touched her, but she did not call him back. Outside, he took a long breath and tried to grin at Haney and failed. He muttered: "It's hell, Bert."

At supper T. Benson met the crew from whiskery Baldy Newt, who had come up the trail from Texas years ago with Haney, on around to handsome young Curly McKay, who made no effort to hide his admiration. They ate with restraint, even waiting for the platter of steak to be passed. Baldy lowered his head so she couldn't see the struggle between his toothless gums and food, and Joe Kerron tried his best to keep his chomping down so she couldn't hear him above the others.

When they had finished Luke's dried apple pie, she said: "Men, I probably should have written Haney that I was a woman, but I didn't know how things were here. It's all right, of course, because, if a woman is going to do what men have done in the past, she's got to put up with what a man does."

"We'll clean the house up," Haney said worriedly.

She shook her head. "No, it's all right. If I planned to live here, I'd build a frame house, but I don't see that much can be done with a dirt shack. Is it the best Uncle Bill could afford?"

"No, ma'am," Haney answered, "but soddies are all right in this country. Warm in winter and cool in summer, and the materials are all around us."

"I can see the materials are all around," she said dryly. "Now I'll tell you men why I came. I intend for this ranch to be run on sound business principles. I expect it to pay me as much profit as it did Uncle Bill."

"It's been dry . . . ," Haney began.

"We'll talk about that later. First I want to tell you cowboys that I'm raising you five dollars a month. I believe in paying better than anybody else. In return, I expect hard work from the best men in the business."

They eyed her dubiously, and, if she had been a less certain woman, she could have sensed their suspicion.

"Maybe you figger on us working twenty hours a day instead of eighteen," Dave said grimly.

"Of course not," she snapped. "Now about this trouble with the nesters. I had a talk with Tucker and Rolf Jaeger before I left town. They both assured me the law is on the side of the nesters, and I'd save trouble if I'd let the nesters cross the river, but I don't agree. It was the cowmen who tamed this country, so I see no justice in handing it over to the farmers."

"It ain't justice for a fact," Haney agreed.

The old man was almost pathetic in his eagerness to please her. Dave's hands fisted. He said: "This country ain't been tamed yet, ma'am."

She looked at him, surprised. "You have an organized county, haven't you?"

"We think we do," Dave answered, "but the county seat's a long ways from here and the sheriff is plumb easy about most things. Nothing but rustling and horse stealing gets him riled."

She seemed puzzled. "What do you suggest about this trouble?"

"I ain't the owner," Dave said sharply.

"I asked you a question."

"Go on," Haney said. "Answer her."

Dave's eyes swung around the table. He knew how the men felt. All he had to do was to keep working on this line and she'd lose every man she had—all but Haney. He reached for tobacco and paper and began rolling a smoke. Haney was the point of the whole thing. If this bull-headed woman got what was coming to her, Haney would be hurt, so Dave surrendered.

"Triangle X, that's the outfit down the river from us, sent to Ogallala for gun hands and put 'em to riding the river. That means a big payroll for men who don't work."

"I can't afford that. What else?"

"Well, we've got Winchesters and ammunition. First time a bunch of nesters crosses the Frenchman, we can shoot the daylight out of 'em."

"That's what you recommend?"

"I ain't in no position to recommend. You're the owner. If that's what you say to do, that's what we'll do, but mostly shooting nesters is like shooting sheep. They ain't fighting men, and they're likely to listen to smart gents like Justin Tucker or Kip Sneed and get into trouble. Besides, they've got women and kids. When you start shooting, they'll get hurt. Then you'll know how it is to have caused the death of decent, hard-working folks who didn't do you no hurt."

He had hoped to turn her to Bert Haney for advice, but he failed. She made no effort to hide her feeling that Haney was finished, that Dave Lanning was the real ramrod of the outfit, and she'd listen to what he said.

"They know what they're doing," she said crisply. "If they get hurt, it's their responsibility. Lanning, your orders are to prevent the nesters crossing the river at any cost. If we have to fight for survival, we'll fight hard."

Dave rose, cigarette drooping from the corner of his mouth, gray eyes frosty. This was the time to tell her what she was and where she could go. But he didn't, for Bert Haney was asking, his voice sharp: "Then it was all right to buy them Winchesters and ammunition?"

She hesitated, biting her lower lip as her eyes swung briefly to Dave's face. He thought she was remembering her words—*I'm not usually sorry for things I do or say.*—but she made no admission of her mistake. She said simply: "Certainly it was all right."

"It's time you got off your knees, Bert," Dave said pointedly, and left the room.

V

The YT hands hunkered in front of the corrals, smoking, while the last of a red sunset went out of the western sky. They had followed Dave when he'd left the table, all but Haney and the cook, Luke Farr. The dusk darkened until it was night. Lightning played along the horizon to the south, and Baldy Newt, always one to talk, said: "We could stand a rain."

No one said anything else. A match glared at the end of the line, lighting a bronze face. Then Haney and Thelma left the cook shack, Thelma calling: "Come over to the office, Lanning!"

"What for?"

"I want to talk to you about ranch business."

"Talk to Bert," Dave said curtly. "He knows more than I do."

She hesitated a moment, the lamplight falling against her tall, strong shape. Her face was shadowed so that Dave could not see her expression. Without another word she whirled and walked rapidly to the house after Haney.

"The way you talk to the owner is a scandal to the hoot owls,"

Curly McKay said. "If it was me, I'd cuddle her up a little."

He was the youngest of the lot, this Curly, and had signed on only the spring before. He liked a pretty face, and Dave had to admit that Thelma's face was pretty enough when she wasn't trying to convince them she was boss.

"I ain't you, Curly," Dave said sharply. "When I cuddle her, it'll be with the palm of my hand."

Curly laughed. "I want to see that when it happens, Dave. She'll fire you."

"Naw," Baldy said, "she's in love with Dave."

They laughed, all but Dave and Curly. Then Joe Kerron said: "Well, I don't reckon I'll be eating YT beans much longer. Guess I'll drift west. You going, Dave? You always said you wanted to see what the Rockies looked like."

Dave tossed his cigarette stub away. "I'd like to see the mountains, all right, Joe."

They knew how it was between him and Haney. All but Curly who got up and kicked viciously at a corral post. "Hang it, Dave, you ain't treating her right. She does own the outfit and you ought to give her time to catch on."

"Give her till Hades cools off," Dave said grimly, "and she wouldn't catch on."

"Somebody's coming," Baldy said.

They rose and stood, listening. A horse was coming from Sunfisher at a hard, reckless pace.

Baldy said: "Don't ride like no nester."

"He ain't coming for fun," Dave said, and started toward the house.

They strung out behind him, uneasiness gripping them.

Curly said: "Maybe it's one of the Triangle X boys. Maybe they've had trouble with Tucker."

"That's the one outfit it wouldn't be," Dave said.

There was a good deal of mystery about Triangle X. It had

been sold the spring before, but nobody on the Frenchman, un-less it was the Triangle X crew, knew who the new owner was. If they did know, they kept silent about it, but whoever he was, he apparently had no scruples about shooting anyone who stepped on Triangle X range. Three nesters had disappeared the month before. Since then Triangle X had not been bothered.

They reached the house, Dave calling: "Bert, somebody's coming in a hurry!"

Haney moved through the doorway. "Traveling all right," he said after a moment.

Thelma pushed by Haney, asking: "What does it mean?"

No one answered. The rider was close now. A moment later the lathered horse was pulled up in the pool of light from the house. The rider was a kid from the livery stable in Sunfisher. He called: "Dave! Nona Tucker sent me to tell you some of them new nesters are crossing the river tonight."

"Where?"

"Two, three miles downstream."

Thelma came to stand beside Dave. "Isn't Nona Justin Tucker's girl?"

"She ain't proud of it," the kid snapped. "Tucker'll beat her for sending me out here." He swung his horse around and headed back to town.

"It's a trap!" Thelma cried. "Can't you see, Lanning? They're waiting out there to murder you."

"Break out them Winchesters," Dave ordered, "and fill your pockets with Thirty-Thirty shells. Curly, give Bert a hand."

They saddled by lantern light, mounted, and stopped briefly in front of the house. Haney and Curly handed out the rifles and ammunition. They checked their handguns and saw that the loops of their belts were filled.

Dave said: "Curly, you and Luke stay here. Blow out the lights and one of you keep awake until we get back."

"Lanning," Thelma burst out furiously, "you've been ignoring me! I tell you it's a trap!"

Dave rode away, the others strung out behind him, and presently the house became dark. There was no sound but the thud of hoofs until Baldy Newt's soft laugh came up the line. "You oughta be ashamed, Dave, ignoring the little gal."

They laughed, all but Dave. He was thinking of Nona, trying to understand why she had done what she had tonight. One thing was clear. She had declared her side, and Justin Tucker did not look like a forgiving man.

The party crossing the river was not hard to find. There were about twenty wagons in the outfit, and, when Dave and his men reined up, three were across. Lanterns made small dots of light on both sides of the Frenchman. Most of the women and children were on the north bank, huddled around the lanterns. The men had double-teamed, for there was a steep pitch on the north side, and the muddy bottom made hard pulling.

None of them paid any attention to the YT men until Dave, rifle held on the ready, asked: "Who's running this outfit?"

A man who had crossed said: "Tucker. He's on the other side."

A wagon was ready to start down the bank when Dave called: "Hold that! You boys that have got over turn around."

Tucker came into the lantern light on the other side, his great head thrown back. "What's the idea, Lanning? You can't keep us from filing on this land."

"Well, now," Dave said, "maybe we can't, but we can sure make a mess out of you while we're trying."

Dave pulled the trigger, the crack of the Winchester sharp in the night silence, the bullet making a geyser of mud at Tucker's feet. He jumped back, yelling: "Are you aiming to kill us?"

"No. I won't have to. You're too smart to stay there."

The nester men gathered behind Tucker, the women and children disappearing into the darkness. Dave's men had lined up along the south bank, their faces grim and hard-visaged in the moonlight. There was this moment of silence while Tucker seemed to be making up his mind.

"Let's talk this over, Lanning," Tucker said finally. "I know you say the sand hills are poor farming ground. We'll have to try it before we're convinced you're right. If you are, we'll leave without making you trouble, but the way things stand now, you don't own the land and therefore you're violating the law when you use force to keep us off the Public Domain."

"What's your interest in this, Tucker?" Dave demanded. "You're no homesteader."

"I have a claim south of Sunfisher," Tucker said mildly. "That makes me a homesteader, and my interest is their interest, but there's more to this than that. I hate monopoly with all my soul, Lanning. Therefore I have dedicated my life to helping honest settlers get what the Homestead Act aimed to provide them with. That's why I'm fighting you and Haney and the rest of the stockmen. Range barons! Cattle kings! Monopolists! Look at you, working for a woman who knows nothing about the cattle business. All she wants is money, money that's taken out of a country that belongs to all of us. Can you defend that system, Lanning?"

He was good with words, this Justin Tucker, but words didn't change the sand hills, nor could politicians passing laws in Congress change what Nature had made. But there was one thing Tucker had said which was true. Dave Lanning was working for a woman who knew nothing of the cattle business, who wanted only money taken from a country belonging to everybody. No, he could not defend that system. Neither could he defend the Triangle X that had imported gun hands who were ready to commit murder.

Because he had no words to match Tucker's, Dave pulled the trigger again, the bullet slapping into the mud within inches of Tucker's feet. He said: "Get 'em back, Tucker. We ain't here to auger. I told you this morning not to have 'em cross unless you wanted to fight."

Tucker raised a fist and shook it at Dave, and his words were heavy with scorn. "All right, Lanning. We'll pull back because we are not prepared to shed blood, but if I had any doubt about what this takes, it's gone now. Kip Sneed said we would have to burn and kill to rid this country of you land thieves. If we must use your tactics, Lanning, be assured that we will."

Maybe Justin Tucker was honest. Tonight he was acting and talking like an honest man, but Dave knew Kip Sneed, and, when Tucker quoted Sneed, it proved that Tucker was either a crook or a gullible fool.

The three wagons on the south side of the Frenchman were turning when the sound of gunfire came to Dave from the direction of the YT buildings. This was what he had feared, the burning and the killing that Sneed had told Tucker was necessary.

"Get 'em back, Tucker!" Dave said, his voice terrible with rage. "And you'd better be out of the country if this is what I think it is!"

Dave swung his horse from the river toward the ranch, fear a spine-tingling chill in him. He couldn't believe Thelma Benson had been right about this being a trap. And he couldn't and wouldn't believe that Nona Tucker had baited it.

They swept back the way they had come, the wind in their faces, the black cloudless sky above them, a great vault freckled by a myriad of stars. Lances of flame from the ranch house probed the darkness. The attacking party had holed up at the corrals and was seemingly content to shoot at the house. A dozen men, Dave guessed.

"Hold your fire until I let go!" Dave shouted, and raced on.

46

The YT assailants must have heard Dave and his men before they swept into the ranch yard, since they ran toward their horses, turning their fire at Dave's party, wild bullets that sang harmlessly overhead. Then Dave and his men cut loose with their Colts. Lead slapped into the barn, splintered corral posts, shrilled away into the night.

There was a moment of confusion before the attackers hit saddles—bucking horses and yelling men and roaring guns. Then they were headed toward the river in full retreat, not even taking time to answer YT's fire.

"Chase 'em to the river!" Dave yelled. "And then come back!" Dave turned toward the house, calling: "Open up, Bert! They're gone!"

"Dave boy!" Haney shouted. "Sure good to hear your voice."

The door opened and Thelma cried: "Why didn't you go after them?"

"The boys'll follow 'em to the river. No use going any farther. Too dark and there's a million places to hide at night. Besides, we'd better stay here."

"Yes, I guess you had," Thelma said coldly. "You ignored me as if I was nobody when I told you it was a trap. Maybe I don't know cows, but I know women and I saw through that Tucker girl."

Haney lighted a lamp. Dave came into the house, resentful eyes turned to Thelma. She was thoroughly angry. Some of her reddish-blonde hair had come unpinned and curled over her forehead. She was downright pretty, Dave admitted, but that wasn't the point. Haney, worried, was looking from one to the other, and Curly McKay, blotting a flow of blood from a bullet slash on his cheek with a wadded bandanna, seemed to be angry enough to swing on Dave.

"You're so danged smart," Curly said, his tone as wicked as a slashing bullwhip, "pulling the boys off and leaving us wide open."

Dave ignored Curly. He said: "Look, ma'am. You ordered us to prevent the nesters crossing at any cost. All right. We turned 'em back. You could hole up here till morning. Take a good bullet to get through a soddy wall."

"Curly got hurt," she flung at him.

"Then he didn't keep his head down," Dave said.

"We had to shoot back, didn't we?" Curly demanded. "How is a man gonna pull a trigger when he keeps his nose in the dirt?"

Dave shrugged. "All right. You had bad luck."

Curly jerked a hand at a window. "I was shooting through there when I got tagged. Could have drilled me between the eyes."

Dave grinned. Curly McKay wasn't fooling anybody. He was backing Thelma, figuring that was one way to get into her good graces.

"Looks like you had good luck," Dave said.

Thelma had been staring at Dave as if she didn't believe what she had heard him say about the nesters. She asked: "Did you really find any settlers?"

"About twenty wagons. Tucker was there, but he listened to reason when I put a bullet under his toes."

"It was still a trap," Thelma said defiantly. "Nona Tucker didn't fool me any. If Justin Tucker is the one who's making our trouble, you can depend on it that the girl was trying to lure you and the men away so those killers could murder me."

Dave turned away, feeling the futility of trying to convince Thelma Benson of anything. There was no point in arguing with her. He heard Haney say apologetically: "You can't blame Dave, ma'am. You said to stop the nesters. He done that, and he didn't have no way of knowing them devils would show up here."

The men had returned, and Baldy Newt was calling: "Dave, we got one of 'em!"

"Dead?" Dave asked, striding toward the corral.

"Dead as he'll ever be," Baldy said. "We dunno who drilled him. Maybe he was hit here, and fell out of his saddle this side of the river."

They had laid the dead man on the ground beside the barn. Dave knelt and, scratching a match, looked at his face: a young man with a wisp of a mustache and long sharp nose. Dave had seen him around town, a loud mouth that had had a lot to say about how the settlers would have to take the law into their own hands.

Thelma had come from the house. She cried out when the match flame showed the nester's face, and backed away. Curly put his arm around her and steadied her. For the first time Dave felt weakness in her, and the knowledge brought a small smile of satisfaction to his lips. He said: "You see, ma'am, talking about killing men and looking at a man who has been killed are two different things."

"She's all right, Dave," Curly said defensively. "She was burning powder same as me and Bert and Luke Farr."

"Then maybe she killed this fellow," Dave said.

"Shut up!" Curly bawled. "Can't you see what you're doing to her?"

Thelma stepped away from Curly. "I'm all right. Yes, Lanning, I may have killed him, but I'm not sorry if I did. He might have killed any of us. Who is he?"

"One of the nesters who's been listening to Kip Sneed and flapping his tongue about running the cattlemen off the Frenchman." Dave scratched his neck thoughtfully. "There's something wrong here. This yahoo was shot in the back and from mighty close up."

"You figger they shot their own man?" Baldy demanded.

"I ain't figgering anything yet," Dave said worriedly, "but it just don't look right. Come sunup, Baldy, you hitch up and take him into town." He wheeled to face Thelma. "Now you can see this ain't no place for a woman. Curly can take you to town in the morning."

"I'm staying right here till this is finished," Thelma blazed. "I'm going to tell Nona Tucker. . . ."

"How come you were so friendly to Tucker and Jaeger in the hotel?" Dave cut in. "You seemed willing to believe 'em when they said I wasn't safe to travel with."

She didn't answer for a moment. When she did, her tone was unusually mild. "I thought they were men of my position. Tucker said he was a judge and Jaeger claimed to be an owner. All right, Dave. I was wrong. Now will you admit you're wrong in trusting Nona Tucker?"

"I guess, ma'am," Dave said in a tone held low, "it'll take a sight more proof than we've got to make me admit that. We don't even know the stable kid was telling the truth when he said she sent him."

"You're in love with her." Thelma stamped her foot in exasperation. "Dave Lanning, you're in love with her, so you won't admit she was trying to murder us."

He ignored what she said. "I keep wondering why you decided you'd ride with me."

"You threatened Jaeger," she cried, "and I didn't want trouble!"

"It wasn't really that, was it?"

She paused, then admitted reluctantly: "No. It was the Tucker girl saying she'd ride with me."

"That's what I thought," Dave said, and turned toward the bunkhouse.

"Wait, Dave," Thelma insisted. "It doesn't prove anything. Maybe she never meant it."

Dave went on, telling himself that Thelma was wrong. He knew the stable kid. He wouldn't lie. Nona had sent him tonight. Dave was sure of that, but he couldn't believe Nona had been a part of a scheme to lure the YT riders away from the ranch. After he had gone to bed and the rest of the hands were asleep, he lay awake, thinking of it and wondering if she really had turned against her father. It was hard to believe she had, but, if he did not believe that, he must believe that Thelma was right.

VI

It was on Thursday that Dave had first brought Thelma Benson to YT. At breakfast Friday morning she said firmly: "I'm here to see the country we claim as our range, Dave. You'll show me around."

There was a shuffling down the long table. Curly McKay stared at her and scowled, but the rest of the men, even Bert Haney, looked down at their plates or took a quick drink of coffee to hide a grin.

"I reckon I'd better keep working," Dave muttered. "You've got to keep doing some things even if you're into a fight up to your neck. Or if the boss comes to look the outfit over."

"What things?" she demanded crisply.

"Things." He got up. "Curly, you show Miss Benson around, but keep your eye peeled and don't get too far from here." He went out quickly, feeling the pressure of Thelma's stare.

They were back at night, not long before dusk, and, when Bert Haney ripped the hide off Curly for keeping Thelma out so long, he hung his head and kicked at the dust.

"You don't need to be so proddy about it," Curly said. "She wouldn't come back. Hod dang it, she is the boss."

"Yeah, and you may be out a boss," Haney returned. "You damned chicken-brained idiot."

Saturday morning Thelma was too stiff to come to breakfast. Dave allowed she could go hungry, that she didn't have any business riding all day and, boss or not, she could walk to breakfast or starve.

"You're a mite rough on her, boy," Bert said reprovingly. "She's a leetle strong-minded, but she ain't afraid. You've got to admit that."

Dave granted something that was unintelligible to Haney and walked off. He wouldn't admit anything about Thelma Benson. She thought she could run a cow outfit like a factory. Sentiment had no place in it. She hadn't said she still thought that, but he knew she did. Anyhow, he couldn't stand her. Sooner or later she'd fire Haney. Maybe she'd make Curly foreman. Curly would be just right for her. He'd carry out all her damned fool orders and say she was doing right.

Dave kept out of her way all day. It would be about like her to *order* him to take her to the dance, and that would just be one too much. This was the night he had a date with Nona. He tried to feel good about it, but something was wrong. Sort of like eating too much cake after he'd been looking forward to a big feed for a month. There were knots in his stomach that wouldn't come out. He knew what it was. All he had to do to get them out was to hear Nona say she hadn't sent the livery stable kid or that she wanted her dad to get tromped on.

He was shaving when Haney came in: "Wipe that lather off, boy. Rolf Jaeger's here, and Thelma says for you to come in."

Dave swung around, his razor poised. "What does he want?"

"You'll find out. Hurry up. I don't like the way things are shaping up."

Dave wiped his face, slipped into a clean shirt, and, grabbing up his gun belt, buckled it around him as he walked to the house. Rolf Jaeger was there, smelling of too much cologne. Thelma was there, too, her hair done up on the back of her head and she'd dabbed on some sweet smelling stuff that reached out and grappled with Jaeger's cologne. She was wearing a new dress, or one Dave hadn't seen, blue silk that fitted her as if it had grown there. For once she didn't seem to have that belligerent look on her face.

"Howdy, Lanning," Jaeger said.

Dave grunted—"Howdy, Jaeger."—and nodded at Thelma. "You wanted me?"

"Yes, Dave. Jaeger has a proposition. I want you to hear it."

"Won't take me long," Jaeger said mildly, his usual small smile on his lips. "I heard you had a raid from the nesters the other night and one of their men was killed. It may be news to you, Lanning, but Tucker considers that after you turned them back from the river the other night, you're asking for violence, so he's planning to give it to you."

"Then we'll give it back," Dave said.

"Be reasonable, Lanning," Jaeger said patiently. "There are two hundred nesters within calling distance. Your men haven't got enough guns to hold off that many."

"I figger we can handle a million nesters. What's your proposition?"

Jaeger shifted his weight in his chair, pale eyes flicking to Thelma and coming back to Dave. "I've been in the cattle business a long time, long enough to see that we're at the end of the open range. From now on there'll be other ways of raising cows. Smaller ranches probably with the rancher owning his range."

"You talk damned funny for a cowman," Dave said bluntly.

"Maybe. You're like most cowmen, so blamed stubborn you'll beat your head against the wave of incoming settlers until it's too late. You were raided the other night. You killed one of their men. It's only a matter of days, perhaps hours, until they'll swarm over the river and wipe you out. Even if you survive this trouble, Tucker will get you when the next election comes up."

Jaeger was almost as cute with words as Justin Tucker, but there was a difference. Tucker sounded as if he believed what he said. Jaeger was trying to convince Thelma that YT was finished, and his words didn't sound right.

"What's the proposition?"

Jaeger shifted his weight again, taking another quick look at Thelma. "It's simple enough, Lanning. I want you to do what I've had to do. Go west. I told you I thought I'd settle here, but I see that's foolish, so I'll move my herd west until I find a place where the nesters aren't pushing. I'll use the open range as long as I can. I'm proposing that you join me." He motioned toward Thelma. "Miss Benson says us cowmen have to work together. I agree, and that's what I'm proposing that we do."

Dave might have believed that Jaeger was on the level if he hadn't been thick with Sneed and Tucker. The trouble was he couldn't see what Jaeger was driving at.

"What do you think?" Thelma asked anxiously. "If Jaeger feels he's licked before he's started, there isn't much hope for us."

"That's the way I feel," Jaeger said as if convinced of the futility of resistance. "I'm here because we're on the same side of the fence, and I felt that by throwing our herds and crews together, we'd be strong enough to defend ourselves on a new range."

"I see." Dave reached for tobacco and paper, eyeing Jaeger. "How come you've been so friendly with Tucker?"

Jaeger tried to look cunning, throwing a quick grin at Thelma. "A case of doing a little spying. I wanted to find out how tough Tucker was and what his settlers were like. I found out. They're different than the rag-tag outfits you see on the trail. They'll fight, Lanning."

"What do you think?" Thelma asked again.

"I ain't the ramrod," Dave answered pointedly. "What about it, Bert?"

"You know what I think," Haney said. "Maybe Jaeger's right about the end of the open range, but I wouldn't run."

"There's your answer, Jaeger," Dave said.

"But it ain't that easy, Dave," Haney said. "You're the one who'll do the fighting, so you're the one who has to make the decision."

"Before you make that decision, Dave," Thelma cut in, "I'd like to have an answer to one question. Jaeger was at the depot when we were jangling about you bringing me out here. He made himself known and later in the hotel dining room he brought Tucker in and introduced him. Now what I want to know is why Jaeger tried so hard to convince me that you were not a man to be trusted?"

"No reason." Jaeger got red in the face. "It's just that Lanning's an *hombre* who likes to fight. You need cooler-headed men, Miss Benson. As for bringing Tucker in, I thought you should meet him since he represents the nesters. After what happened the other night, you can see how far they will go under his leadership."

Dave took a long breath. Several things fell into place. He asked softly: "So you want us to throw in with you?"

"That's right. Have your boys gather your beef and bring the herd down to the river. I'll send for my outfit. You can hold your bunch here till we bring ours up."

Dave drew his gun and eared back the hammer. "Damn you for a sneaking, lying thief, Jaeger. Get on your horse and drift before I let daylight through your hide."

Jaeger reared up out of his chair, his face white. "Now, wait. . . ."

"Git," Dave said. "If I ever meet up with you again, you'd better reach."

Jaeger did get. Not even glancing at Thelma, Jaeger swung into the saddle, and left the yard in a wild run. Haney laughed softly. "I wondered how long you'd stand for it, Dave."

"I don't understand," Thelma said.

"I don't know the game," Dave admitted, "but Jaeger gave himself away when he said for us to gather our herd. Wouldn't be no trouble to steal all of 'em if we had 'em right here waiting for 'em. Maybe they'd bust in here and chouse 'em across the Colorado line. It was too thin, him saying you needed cooler-headed men and all that hogwash. He knew Bert was past riding, so he did his best to get you down on me, knowing I was the gent who'd be most likely to start cracking a few caps. Now I'm going to town to have a talk with Tucker. I've got a hunch that Jaeger's fooled him just like he's been trying to fool you."

"I suppose you'll see the Tucker girl," Thelma said as if she thoroughly disapproved of it.

"Yeah, I figger on it."

"It seems to me a very foolish thing to be so friendly with our enemies, especially after the way she sent that message. . . ."

"I don't reckon I'll listen to that," Dave broke in. "Not till we know Nona did what you claim she did."

Thelma rose, her face very sober. "I know I'm stubborn, Dave, and perhaps a little blind, but so are you. From the time I came, Haney has been telling me what a good man you are to be foreman. You're wrong, but I've decided you'll do. From today on, you're running YT. Don't. . . ."

"Wait a minute. You're wanting me to ramrod this outfit?"

"That's exactly what I said. Now, if you'll sit down. . . ."

"No ma'am." Dave Lanning had never been as thoroughly

56

angry in his life as he was at this moment. He had told her what he'd do if she hurt Bert Haney, but now he knew he couldn't do it. He said evenly: "You run your outfit just like you want it run. I'm finished. You coming, Bert?"

Haney's leathery face was tight and drawn. "I'm surprised at you, Dave. I never figgered you'd run out on a fight."

"And I never thought you'd git down on your knees and stick your nose into the dirt like you've done for a stuck-up, mule-headed woman like she is."

Dave swung out of the room, knowing he couldn't stay, or he'd say more than he should. He packed his stuff, threw gear on his horse, and within fifteen minutes he was on the road to Sunfisher, not even looking back at the house. The past was gone, cut away from him in one clean sharp stroke, leaving only the memories. He felt a growing prickle of uneasiness. Conscience, he thought. He was running out on Bert Haney, but he couldn't blame himself. There was only so much any man could stand and he had stood more than that since Thelma Benson had come to Sunfisher.

If Bert wanted to lower his pride and hang around YT after what had happened, it was his business, but that wasn't Dave Lanning's way. He'd have his date with Nona Tucker and ride on—west where he could see trees on the mountains, something besides the flat lands with the eternal buffalo grass. His mind lingered on Nona and he wondered if she would go with him.

VII

It was dusk when Dave rode into Sunfisher and stabled his mount. The wagon train, he saw, was gone. Moved on west, he thought. The business at the river had been enough to convince them that there was no room on the Frenchman for them.

Dave had a drink in the Idle Hour, surprised that no one else was in the saloon. It was a little early for the usual Saturday night crowd of cowboys who rode in from miles around, but for weeks the streets had been thronged all day and evening with nesters, most of them stopping off on their way to the new land they aimed to claim. Now there was just Dave and the droopy-eyed barkeep.

"What happened to the sodbusters?" Dave asked.

"Hanged if I know," the barman answered. "An hour or so ago the place was full. You'd have had a fight on your hands the minute you poked your nose into the place."

Dave grinned. A fight would be to his liking except that he might not be in any shape to take Nona to the dance. He asked: "What were they on the prod about?"

"They ain't forgot the boy you plugged the other night. Shoving 'em back across the river didn't help." The barman shook his head and wiped at a puddle, narrowed eyes on Dave. "The loco thing about it is that all of a sudden these grangers turned on Tucker. They've been claiming he was the smartest gent that ever pulled on a pair of pants. Now they claim he's yellow and they'll run him out of the country if he don't go himself."

Dave scratched his head. That made less than sense. Tucker, with his fine words and an innate sense of leadership, had been accepted as the man to make their decisions. Dave poured himself another drink. "Abe, you must be off your noggin. Been drinking too much of your red-eye. Most of these sodbusters allow that Tucker oughta be President."

The barman snorted. "Dave, they wouldn't run him for dog-catcher. Sneed's their man now. Why, Tucker ain't even been on the street since the middle of the afternoon. Seems like he was trying to hold 'em back and all they want to do is fight. A while ago Jaeger rode in, his horse all lathered up, and right away Sneed says we'll cross the river at sunup and we'll clean every YT cow off the sand hills. I heard him say that when he was standing right there."

Dave stared at the barman, forgetting his drink. It was making sense in a way he didn't like. Jaeger hoped to talk Thelma into gathering her cattle, but it hadn't worked. When that had failed, Sneed had started working the nesters up.

"Sneed's a big windbag," Dave said uneasily. He stared down at the amber liquor, asking himself why he should be worrying about it. The YT troubles weren't his any more. Thelma Benson could do her own worrying. He was free as a bird. He'd dance with Nona tonight, ask her to marry him, and, if she said no, he'd ride on. Maybe he wouldn't even ask her to marry him. If a man was going to see what was on the other side of the Rockies, he'd better travel alone. Sure, that was the thing to do. He'd dance with Nona and then ride on and forget her.

But he knew he wouldn't. The barman kept eyeing him as if he was expecting something. Finally Dave said: "What's the matter with you, Abe? You're looking at me like I'd started herding sheep."

"I can't figger it out," the barkeep said worriedly. "Either you're sick or you're crazy. What are you hanging around here for?"

"I quit the YT. Ain't none of my troubles no more."

"So you quit when the fighting was getting ready to start," the apron said scornfully. "Now I know you're sick. Look, you. . . ." The barman choked, suddenly afraid to say what he had intended to. "All right, Dave. It ain't none of your business. Sneed'll hang Bert. Maybe shoot every YT man they catch, and Nona Tucker is out there trying to stop 'em."

"Now you're crazy. She wouldn't. . . ."

"The devil she ain't. Old Justin's up there in his hotel room shaking in his boots, but Nona left town half an hour ago. She was headed. . . ."

Dave didn't wait to hear. He went out of the saloon on the run, poked his head into the archway of the stable, told the hostler to saddle up two of the best horses he had, and raced on down the boardwalk to the hotel. He didn't like the idea of not riding his own horse, but he needed a fresh animal.

"What room has Tucker got?" Dave asked the clerk.

"Twenty-Eight. Say, Dave, Tucker's girl left here. . . ."

Dave took the stairs three at a time and ran down the hall until he came to room 28. He tried the knob, found the door locked, and, backing away, smashed it open with a blow of his boot. Tucker was on the bed, a gun at his side. He jumped up, grabbing at the Colt, but he had no chance to fire. Dave was on him, twisting his wrist and making him drop the gun.

"Come on, Tucker," Dave said. "We're going after Nona."

Tucker wiped a hand across his face. It was then that Dave saw the bruises that marred his cheeks and jaw, the puffy lips, the right eye that was nearly closed.

"I can't go," Tucker muttered. "They'll kill me."

"What happened to you?"

"Sneed beat daylight out of me." He looked up at Dave, suddenly rebellious. "I can't go, Lanning. They won't hurt Nona, but they'll lynch me if I go out there. I tried to stop them. Nona's right, but I've been blind. Sneed and Jaeger have been working on their own thieving scheme and they don't give a hang about the settlers."

Dave picked up Tucker's gun and slipped it into his waistband. "You're going with me, Tucker. You'd be better off if they did lynch you than if you sit around and hate yourself because you let Nona do what you should have done."

For a moment Tucker stood in indecision, rubbing his bruised face, pride fighting his fear. Then he said: "All right, Lanning. I'll go, but neither one of us will come back."

He went out then, Dave behind him.

After they were in their saddles and headed west, Dave asked:

"Where did Nona go?"

"Johnson's Spring. That's where the wagon train that just got in moved to, and Sneed's sent out word for the other settlers to come in. They aim to move before dawn and attack your ranch."

"What changed you, Tucker?" Dave asked. "When we stopped you at the river, you were giving us Sneed's talk about burning and killing to rid the country of land thieves."

For a moment Tucker made no answer. Then he said: "I finally had it beaten through my head that Nona was right. She said that when we teamed up with crooks to accomplish our purpose, we were as bad as the crooks. I didn't think so because we needed Sneed and Jaeger to drive you out of the country."

"What's Jaeger and Sneed after?"

"Your cattle. There's a big railroad construction job being started across in Colorado. That means a market for beef. Sneed has a bunch of men waiting at the state line. We were supposed to stampede your cattle that far and his men would pick them up."

It might work exactly as Sneed had planned it. Jaeger would be his front, posing as a cowman the same as he posed before the nesters and before Thelma Benson, and Sneed would have his experienced butchers waiting to take over the YT herd when it crossed the line.

"So you were in it," Dave said contemptuously. "The trouble was you'd convinced your grangers that the thing to do was to kill us and drive our cattle out of the country. When you changed your mind, you couldn't swing 'em back."

"That's it," Tucker agreed. "I didn't know about the raid Sneed made on the YT. We were honestly trying to cross the river, but we wouldn't have done it had we known Sneed was taking advantage of the opportunity to attack your place when you and your boys were gone."

"It was Nona that sent word what you were doing."

61

"She didn't know what Sneed was up to," Tucker said quickly. "What she's been after all the time was to break us with Sneed and Jaeger."

The fires of the settlers' camp showed ahead now, the great bulks of the covered wagons vague shadows before them. Horsemen were ahead, moving toward the camp; others were riding in from the north. Two hundred, Jaeger had claimed, and he had been right when he had said there weren't enough YT guns to hold them off. If all the stockmen on the Frenchman were co-operating, the nesters could be held north of the river, but Triangle X had never wanted to co-operate on anything.

Now Dave gave thought to this, a vague suspicion taking root in his mind. None of the other ranchers were on good terms with Triangle X, and the gun crew that had been imported from Ogallala never came to town. The more Dave thought about it, the more his suspicions seemed to make sense. If the nesters, under Jaeger's and Sneed's leadership, were able to wipe YT out, it would be simple enough for Triangle X to sweep in from the east and occupy YT range before the nesters staked their claims, and there would be no evidence that Triangle X had anything to do with the trouble. Cattle would simply be driven onto a range that had been vacated, and the nester wave would be beaten back by the Triangle X.

Dave had no plan in mind. He would not know what he could do until he was there, facing Sneed and Jaeger and the settlers, but there was one more thing he needed to know.

"What changed you over so you agreed with Nona and made you try to hold the settlers back?" Dave asked.

"I didn't get back to town till noon and I didn't know about the raid till then. That was when I heard about Charley Morgan being shot. I knew him well in Iowa. A gabby kid, but he'd have been all right if he'd had a chance to grow up. Right then I saw what would happen if we kept going. A dozen men would be killed, men who had families to support, and there wasn't any sense to it because there's a million acres west of here where they could settle. I tried to tell them that, but Sneed stopped me by beating me up."

The chances were they wouldn't listen to Tucker now, Dave thought, for Justin Tucker had quit when he'd been beaten, and that meant he was finished. There was no place on the Frenchman for a man who had quit.

They rode through the circle of wagons and reined up. Then a long breath broke out of Tucker and he gripped Dave's arm.

"Look, Lanning. Look at that."

There must have been a hundred men around the fire in the center of the circle and more were coming in, but it wasn't the men who had attracted Tucker's attention. It was Nona, who held a Winchester on the ready. She was facing Rolf Jaeger, and there was no mistaking the purpose that was in her.

"Tell them the truth, Jaeger!" Nona cried. "Tell them they're being used to murder and steal so that you and Sneed can fill your pockets!"

"Wait a minute, Tucker," Dave breathed. "She's doing all right."

The next minute he saw he was wrong, for a man had slipped behind Nona and gripped her arms at her sides, holding her so that she could not move. Dave handed Tucker his gun, plucked his own, and ran toward Nona, knowing that time was short.

"That's better," Jaeger was saying. "I don't talk good with a gun in my face. Take her away, Larson. Now, folks, I'll tell you the truth."

"He won't tell you the whole truth!" Tucker shouted.

Other men in the fringe of the crowd wheeled when they heard Tucker's voice and drew guns. One of them called: "Stand where you are, Tucker! We're done listening to you."

"Look at him!" Jaeger shouted. "If you've got any doubt of

where Tucker stands or that he's sold out, you shouldn't have now. He's brought a YT man."

"Here's the cowboys!" Sneed shouted. "You settlers take care of YT. Then there'll be nobody to stop you from crossing the Frenchman."

Dave dropped his gun into holster and moved toward the center of the circle. It was then that he recognized the gunslicks who had followed Sneed. They were the killers Triangle X had imported from Ogallala, and the vague suspicion that had been in his mind grew into what seemed a certainty. It was his guess that Jaeger owned the Triangle X.

VIII

There, in the smoky light of the fire, Dave faced Rolf Jaeger and Kip Sneed, and he sensed the triumph each of them felt. There was no other man on the Frenchman they would rather have their hands on than Dave Lanning.

"I'm right glad to see you boys," Dave said, and moved into the circle, Tucker reluctantly following.

"Well, boys," Sneed was saying, "I told Tucker to keep away from here, but he didn't figger I meant it. Now I say to hang him and Lanning."

A growl of approval rose from a hundred throats. Nona screamed: "Don't do it, you fools! Lanning's the best friend you've got!"

Sneed laughed. "Hear the girl, boys? Lanning's our friend."

"That's right," Dave said, "and I'll prove it if you'll listen. You're honest men who have been fooled into thinking you've got to be thieves and killers the same as Jaeger and Sneed. If you are honest, you will listen."

"We've listened to Tucker," a settler cried, "and what did it get us? He says we've got to fight. Then he swings around and tells us to keep going west. I've gone far enough, mister."

64

"That was before I saw Charley Morgan's body!" Tucker shouted. "You know what it means if we fight."

"A little slow thinking of that," Sneed jeered. "I say it's worth any price you pay if you get homes. Ain't that what you came here for?"

"Your land's waiting," Jaeger said. "Let's get started."

"Stand pat," Dave said. "Maybe you'll hang me when I'm done, but before you do, I aim to say my piece."

"We'll listen, and then we'll do the hanging," a settler said. "I saw Charley Morgan's body, too, and I figger that stringing you up will help square his killing."

"Take more'n that!" another yelled. "Charley was shot in the back!"

Dave remembered that. Shot in the back and up close. "Who do you reckon shot him?" Dave demanded. "Who was with him?"

"His friends," Jaeger said quickly. "There ain't no augering about who shot him. You've got nothing to say. . . ."

"I said we'd swap smoke, Jaeger," Dave cut in. "We'll do it now, if you keep flapping your tongue." He waved a hand toward the settlers' bearded faces, bronzed faces, these men who had brought their families to a wild land because of the driving hunger to own their homes. "I've got one thing to ask you boys. Sneed said you were to take care of YT. That means murder. How will you feel the rest of your life knowing you got your start by killing a woman?"

"What woman?" a settler asked.

"Thelma Benson, owner of the YT. She was there when you men raided the ranch. Which ones of you were in the raid?"

There was a stirring among them as men looked at their neighbors and a shaking of heads.

"What difference does it make?" Jaeger demanded. "I tell you we're wasting time."

"Maybe," a settler said, "but I kind of like to hear what this cowhand's got to say. I knowed Charley Morgan was in that fight . . . but I don't know of another settler who was."

"I'll tell you who was in it," Dave said. "Jaeger and that bunch of gun-throwing toughs that walked in behind Sneed. And I'll tell you who shot your man, Morgan. It was Jaeger or one of his men. None of us got close enough to burn his coat with the shot."

"Why would Jaeger do that?" someone demanded.

"You know the scheme," Dave flung at the questioner. "Wipe out YT and drive our cattle into Colorado. That was Sneed's profit. Yours was to get the land but where is Jaeger's? I'll tell you. Triangle X is east of YT. You drive us out and Triangle X moves in. Why? Because Jaeger owns Triangle X. Why else would Triangle X gun dogs be here now? Why else would they have pulled off the raid?"

"He's lying!" Jaeger shouted. "My outfit is Skull, like I told you. I'm moving into Colorado."

"That don't account for Triangle X men being here now!" Dave shouted. "That's the truth Nona Tucker wanted you boys to hear. You're doing their killing for 'em, but you won't get the land because Triangle X will move in."

"Makes sense!" a nester called. "I ain't fixing to do nobody's killing."

"That's why Charley Morgan was murdered by the men he rode with!" Dave cried. "To get you mad enough to fight YT. A big fight like this will bring the sheriff in, and who was to wipe us out? You boys, and you'd hang for it, but Sneed and the YT cows and Triangle X's tough gun hands would be over the line into Colorado. Then the regular Triangle riders would chouse their cows onto YT range."

It was Jaeger who made the first move, right hand blurring down for his gun. Dave caught that first hint of motion and went for his Colt. It was close, so close that the two tongues of flame seemed to have licked out to meet each other, the gun thunder melting into one burst of sound. Rolf Jaeger went down, breaking at knee and hip, and he fell with one arm stretched out before him as if trying to retrieve his gun.

Some of the settlers broke for cover. Larson, still holding Nona, pulled her away into the darkness, but Justin Tucker, who had been afraid, was the one who held some of the settlers there to fight. He screamed: "Jaeger wouldn't have started it if he hadn't been guilty!"

Dave was hit. He bent forward, laboring for breath. He saw Sneed jerk his gun from his holster, and he laced a bullet into the big man's chest. Then he fell, his right side numb. As he lay there, guns hammered out their thunder, and lead screamed above him. Blood spread along his ribs and weakness was in him. He tried to sit up, tried to lift his gun from the ground, but the strength was not in him.

It was hours later that Dave came to. He was, he saw, in a bed in the Sunfisher hotel, and the doctor was working on him. Nona Tucker was holding a lamp close to his side for the medico to see. Dave shifted and heard a distant sound that must have been his voice, and he passed out again.

It was dark when he awoke. His head was clear. He lay for a time with his eyes on Nona, who was sitting beside his bed, and again he thought how much she looked like an angel.

Reaching out, he took her hand. "Don't you ever sleep?"

Startled, she looked up, not knowing until he had spoken that he was conscious. "Not lately, but I can now." She rubbed her head as if she was very tired. "Dave, Thelma Benson has been waiting to see you."

He stared at Nona, his mind gripping all that had happened. He said: "I don't want to see her. I'm done with YT."

"No, Dave. Talk to her."

"All right." He clenched his fists above the blanket.

Nona crossed the room and opened the door. She called— "Thelma."—and stepped aside as Thelma Benson walked in. She was dressed for traveling.

"I'm taking the night train, Dave," Thelma said. "I wanted see you before I left. I told you I was not usually sorry for things I do or say. That's right, but everything that has happened to me since I got here has been unusual. I'm wrong about there being no sentiment in the cattle business. I guess that's the big thing that's between us. I need you to run YT. You can't turn me down again. You see, Bert is in bad shape. I'm taking him with me to Omaha to a specialist. It's his stomach. Maybe nothing can be done, but I want to do all I can for him. How about it, Dave?"

He looked up at her, suddenly realizing how she felt about him, and knowing that, if it wasn't for Nona, things might be entirely different. He said: "I'll be back on YT as soon as I can."

She smiled. "Thank you, Dave. Since I've been here, I've learned more in less time than I ever learned before in my life. From now I'll take the YT's profit and losses without arguing."

She went quickly from the room. Then Nona was beside him.

"The settlers?" he asked.

"The ones who don't have claims are moving on. There won't be any more trouble with them."

He reached for her hand and pulled her down to him. He kissed her, and, when she drew away, he said: "I always had the notion I wanted to see some mountains, but I guess this is my country, if it suits you."

"I'm a flatlander myself, Dave," she told him. "This country suits me fine."

★ ★ ★ ★ ★

FIGHTING MAN

★ ★ ★ ★ ★

I

Following the Stone Saddle cattle trail, Tully Bain topped the summit, and by the middle of the afternoon reached the spring that gave birth to Whetstone Creek. He dismounted and watered his black gelding, thinking that this morning the three years he had been gone had seemed an eternity. Now that he was within five miles of Starbuck they seemed a short time.

He built a fire, shivering a little in the sharp May air. As he took the fire-blackened coffee pot down from a stub of a pine limb, he thought of the countless times he had used this same pot. It had hung there from the first summer that cattle had been driven from Bowstring Valley into the Blue Mountains; he had used it along with Ed and Lon Dorsey and even the Knapps before the trouble had started.

He fried bacon and ate, puzzling over why his friend, Bob Hoven, the Bowstring County sheriff, had sent for him. Hoven was not a man who would ordinarily ask for help. Then he put it out of his mind, his thoughts turning to the half interest in Broken Bell he had given up and now wanted to reclaim; he thought of Beth Carradine and wondered if she still had any feeling for him.

Tully started to reach for the coffee pot when the crack of a rifle splintered the mountain silence, the bullet sending the pot kiting off the fire, coffee sizzling as it poured out of a hole near the bottom. Instinct drove Tully away from the fire in a lunge for cover. He heard a boisterous guffaw and a shout: "Take it easy, Bain!"

Tully stood motionlessly, hand on his gun butt, trying to identify the voice. He had heard it often enough, but three years had blurred his memory so it was a moment before he remembered. It was a gunman, Matt Quinn, who rode for the Knapps.

"You're a blamed poor shot, Matt!" Tully called.

Quinn's stubby body showed above a windfall pine on the slope to the east. "That slug went right where I wanted it to," he bragged, and walked toward the spring. "You should've seen the look on your mug just now. Reminded me of last Fourth of July when Pete tossed a firecracker under Ed Dorsey's horse. Never laughed so hard in my life."

It would be like Pete Knapp to throw a firecracker, and it would be like Quinn to laugh. Tully kept his hand on his gun butt, watching Quinn who was holding his Winchester on the ready. The gunman eyed him, the laughter leaving his pale blue eyes. He was a killer and fanatically loyal to Rocky and Pete Knapp, two facts that were at least partly responsible for their brutal arrogance.

"How's things on the Box K?" Tully asked.

"Been a long winter," Quinn answered, "and the grass is slow starting."

He might have added that the Knapps still wanted Broken Bell. It was a miracle they didn't have it. Ed Dorsey was no scrapper and his son Lon was a pale copy of his father. Tully said: "Get your horse and I'll ride into Starbuck with you."

"I reckon not," Quinn said blandly. "Rocky sent me up here to head you back over the mountains."

"How'd Rocky know I was coming?"

"Why, I guess he just listened to the leaves rustle."

"Looks like you'd have been waiting on the stage road."

"Carl Lytell's over there." Quinn waggled his rifle barrel at

Tully. "Folks always said you was born a bad one like your old man. We've heard some yarns about you turning out to be a gunslinger. Me, I like to test a man who works up a reputation for hisself, but Rocky, he says no."

"I'm not going back," Tully said. "I've got a half interest in Broken Bell."

"Which is nothing. Broken Bell's busted. Ed Dorsey's in debt to Judge Carradine up to his ears." Quinn grinned. "Funny thing about Broken Bell cows. They've quit having calves."

"And maybe Box K cows have twins."

Quinn winked. "Mebbeso. Well, I've got to ride over and tell Carl I seen you. Ain't no skin off my nose if you're bound to keep going and get a dose of lead colic."

Turning, Quinn climbed the side of the cañon and presently Tully heard him ride away. Tully kicked out his fire and, mounting, went on down the trail to Starbuck. He thought of his last bitter talk with Ed Dorsey. The Knapps had been pushing even then and Tully had known it was time to make a stand.

"They'll behave if we ride over there and burn a little powder," Tully had urged.

"And get ourselves shot!" young Lon Dorsey had shouted.

Ed, a gray, gentle man, had nodded somberly. "I figure we'd best just try to get along with 'em."

"Then the devil with you!" Tully had cried. "I'm getting out!"

He had been twenty then. Now, looking back, he could make a cool judgment of himself. He'd been a brash kid and no mistake. He'd stopped at the Carradine house in town and asked Beth to marry him, to ride away with him.

"I can't leave Dad," she'd said. "I wouldn't go anyway. If you love me, you'd settle down and work and save your money."

He'd left then, angry and hurt and bitter because she hadn't understood. The only thing he'd been proud of was the memory of his father Red Bain, who had been Ed's partner. Ed had raised Tully after Red had been killed in a gunfight in Starbuck, and, although Ed had liked Tully's father, he had seldom mentioned him.

There were still a few old-timers in Starbuck who talked about Red Bain and the wild things he had done. The stories had grown with the telling until he had become a sort of legend, and folks seemed to expect the same things from Tully. But spinning yarns about a tough hand who had died years ago was one thing, having another one grow up among them was something else, so people had started calling Tully a bad one.

Tully rode out of the pines and within the hour reached Starbuck, a small town located at the junction of Bowstring and Whetstone Creeks. The valley stretched far to the south, rimrock making a blurred line against a sky that had been swept clear of clouds.

Three years had not changed Starbuck's false fronts and dust and hitch poles with a dozen horses tied to them. Of the few dwellings scattered aimlessly in the sagebrush, Judge Carradine's brick house was the only one that made the slightest pretense at dignity.

Tully reined into the livery stable and stepped down. The hostler swore softly when he recognized Tully. He said: "Hanged if it ain't young Bain."

"It's me right enough," Tully said.

"You've come back at a devil of a bad time," the hostler said bitterly. "Rocky Knapp's walking big and proud. You can lay it to Judge Carradine. Sold out to Rocky, damn his soul."

For a moment Tully didn't move, his lanky body arrow straight, gray eyes searching the old man's gaunt face. "Say that over, Jeff . . . slow like."

"Don't make sense, knowing the judge like you done," the hostler said, "but it's true."

Jeff led the black down the runway to the horse trough behind the stable. Tully caught up with him, asking: "What about the judge?"

"The little fellers like the Dorseys are getting the dirty end of the stick, that's what. Now with the sheriff gone, I dunno what'll happen."

Tully gripped the old man's skinny arm. "What happened to Bob?"

"Disappeared. Murdered, I reckon, and his body hid. The Knapps didn't want a straight sheriff, so I figure they got rid of Bob."

"What's the judge done?"

"Loaned a lot of money. Now he's closing everybody out, the Dorseys and all of 'em."

Jeff turned his back, so angry he couldn't talk. Wheeling, Tully strode down the alley and across a vacant lot to the Carradine house. Jeff was wrong about the judge. He had to be. Carradine wasn't that kind of a man.

II

Tully stepped up on the Carradine porch and yanked the bell pull, hearing the metallic jangle far inside the big house. The blinds were lowered at all the front windows, giving a chilled, inhospitable appearance to the house.

Now, waiting uneasily, Tully wondered how Beth would receive him. He was still in love with her and he always would be. When he'd left, he had thought she loved him, but that had been three years ago, and they had parted in anger.

The massive oak door swung open and Carradine stood there, bloodshot eyes pinned coldly on Tully as if he were a complete stranger. And Tully, staring at Carradine, found it hard to believe that three years could change a man so much.

The judge was about sixty, but he looked older. He was a tall man, completely bald, with heavy, black brows jutting out over

75

dark eyes. It was the only familiar thing about him. His bony face was thin, almost cadaverous, his yellow skin as lifeless as old leather, his mouth a brown, unfriendly line across his face.

"Howdy, Judge," Tully said.

Carradine peered at him through steel-rimmed glasses that had slipped far down on his long nose. He stepped outside and closed the door. "I heard you were coming back," he said harshly. "Well, we don't need your kind in Bowstring Valley. Keep riding."

Tully, staring at the judge's barren face, could not say anything for a moment. This was not the Judge Carradine he had known and respected; he was a stranger, or perhaps the ghost of a man whose soul had died.

"I want to see Beth," Tully said.

"Get out of town and leave her alone," Carradine snapped. "She's going to marry Pete Knapp."

Tully felt as if Carradine had struck him with a club. He said: "You must be crazy to say that."

"I'm the sanest men in Bowstring County. I won't live long, but I aim to live long enough to see her married to a man who can take care of her."

"He'd make life hell for her. You. . . ."

"I love Beth," Carradine insisted. "I love her so much I won't let her suffer the way she did after you left. She cried for a week. She . . . she. . . ." He threw out a hand in a gesture of agony. "Leave her alone."

Tully hesitated, thinking bleakly he could never forgive himself if he had brought that kind of grief to her. He turned and would have walked away if the door had not been flung open.

"Tully!" Beth cried, and ran past her father to him.

He wheeled back and caught her in his arms. She had thrown herself at him. Her arms were around him and she clung to him, kissing him with the wild abandon of a woman who was clutching at something she had lost and was determined never to lose it again.

"Beth!" Carradine screamed. "Go back into the house."

She drew her mouth away from Tully's and looked at him, her full lips parted. He could not doubt the love that was in her round, hazel eyes, but there was something else, too, something he could not identify at the moment. She turned, tucking his arm through hers. "Isn't it wonderful to have him back, Dad?"

They walked toward Carradine, and, when they were a step away, he whirled and ran down the carpeted hall.

"He's going after his gun," Beth said as she led Tully into the house and opened a door into the living room. "Stay out of sight."

"He's crazy as a bed bug," Tully said. "What happened?"

"I don't know," she said. "Not all of it." She pushed him into the living room and shut the door.

Carradine was coming back along the hall. Tully opened the door a crack. He heard the old man ask: "Has he gone?"

"No," she answered. "Dad, I made the wrong decision once. I won't make it again on account of you."

Carradine was opposite the door by then. Tully slammed it open and drove at Carradine who turned toward him, cursing. He fired, the bullet snapping past Tully's head to rip into oak paneling, then Tully had him by the wrist, twisting it until Carradine cried out in pain and dropped the gun.

"Now maybe we can talk," Tully said. "Peaceable." He picked up Carradine's gun and slid it into his waistband. "I ain't gonna hurt you, Judge. I just want to know. . . ."

Carradine's eyes were glazed. Now his knees buckled and he went back against the wall and on down to the floor. Beth knelt beside him and felt for his pulse. "He's fainted, Tully. Carry him to his room."

Tully picked up Carradine, the limp body light in his arms, and followed Beth up the stairs and into a bedroom. He laid the old man on the lace spread that covered the bed. He asked: "How did he hear I was coming back?"

"I've been getting Bob's mail. I lost your letter and he found it." She stared down at her father, fighting back her tears. She whispered: "I love him, Tully, but I wish he was dead. I . . . I guess that's wicked, but it's the way I feel."

"I heard Bob had disappeared, but, if you've been getting his mail, you must know where he is."

"Come down to the kitchen and I'll tell you while I finish supper."

He followed her into the hall, his gray eyes on her. She had changed, but it was the natural change that three years brings to a girl who has become a woman. Her body had rounded out; her pink house dress fitted snugly over breasts and hips. He remembered how her rebellious brown hair had never seemed in place, but now it was neatly pinned at the back of her head.

"I should apologize for the way I greeted you," she said. "I mean, we can't just pick up where we left off."

"I was hoping you'd greet me that way," he said.

She smiled wryly. "But for all I know, you're married. I need you, Tully, but I wouldn't steal another woman's man."

"I'll never be another woman's man," he said.

She took his arm. "Come on. I know you're hungry."

They went down the stairs together and on into the kitchen, Tully tossing his hat on the table, suddenly realizing he was both tired and hungry, and uneasy over the situation he had found. The sun was almost down now. Beth lighted a lamp and stoked up the fire.

Tully rolled a cigarette and sat down at the table, watching Beth while she worked at the stove. Without turning to look at him, she said: "Old man Knapp died just before you left. After that Rocky and Pete got worse. They want everything and Bob was in their way, although he couldn't do much because nobody would help him. Five men have been murdered since you left. Bob did all he could, but he just couldn't get any evidence against the Knapps."

She whirled to face him. "It happened two weeks ago. He'd been out to Broken Bell, trying to track some cows that had been stolen from the Dorseys, but he lost the trail in that lava bed west of the valley. Two men jumped him a little ways from town. They were masked, but it must have been Lytell and Quinn. They beat him up. Almost killed him."

Swinging back to the stove, she forked meat into a platter. "He tapped on my window and I helped him get to his house. He's been there ever since. Nobody but me knows he's in town. I knew he had your address, so I got him to write to you."

She brought food to the table. Tully didn't say anything. There was nothing to say. It was hard to believe that Bob Hoven was hiding in his house like a scared kid. Not the Bob Hoven Tully remembered.

"We'll go over there as soon as we eat," she said.

"Is he all right?"

"No. He wouldn't let me get Doc Wallace, but Doc wouldn't have done him any good." She sat down and looked at Tully defiantly. "But you can't blame him unless you've been through what he has."

Tully began to eat, knowing then that it was not Bob Hoven's bodily injuries that kept him in the house. It was beyond understanding. How could it happen to a man who had once possessed great courage?

III

When they finished, Beth said: "I'll look in on Dad before we go."

Tully remained at the table, staring blankly at his plate. He had respected Bob Hoven more than any other man he had ever known, respected him for his judgment and integrity and courage. Hoven had taught him how to use a gun, and, if Tully had not been taught, he would not have lived to return to the valley.

Hoven had never told him he was born to be bad. Instead, he'd said: "It's what's inside a man that counts. You make the pattern for your life, Tully. Nobody makes it for you."

Beth returned a moment later. "Dad's all right," she said.

As they left the house, Tully asked: "How did Furnes happen to let you have Bob's mail?"

Furnes had been one of the first settlers in the valley along with Carradine and Ed Dorsey and Tully's father. He had the only store in Starbuck and was the postmaster, a shriveled, stubborn old man who seldom changed his mind about anything.

"I had to tell him Bob had been wounded and was waiting to get well. I said he needed his mail."

When they reached Hoven's back door, Beth tapped three times, paused, then tapped again. The lock grated as it turned, and the door swung in, Hoven making a vague shadow before them. He said: "Come in."

"Tully's here," Beth said.

They went in, Beth shutting and locking the door. Hoven lighted a lamp and, turning to Tully, held out his hand. "I'm glad to see you, boy," he said. "Real glad."

Tully gripped his hand. Except for the scars on the lawman's face, there was no apparent change in him. The blue eyes, the red, unruly hair, the freckles on his snub nose, all were as Tully remembered. He was relieved, for he had been afraid he'd find a trembling wreck of a man.

Hoven motioned to a chair. "Sit down."

Tully took the chair, glancing around the familiar kitchen. He had eaten many meals here, often talking with Hoven far into the night. Now, thinking about those talks, Tully found it harder than ever to believe Hoven was hiding. He still carried his gun; the star was pinned to his shirt. Then Tully thought of the lamplight and, glancing at the windows, saw that several layers of blankets covered them.

"I'll bring you something to eat after Dad's asleep," Beth said.

Hoven nodded absently, eyes on Tully's face. He asked: "Why did you come back?"

"You sent for me."

"It would take more'n that," Hoven said impatiently.

Tully glanced at Beth who pulled up a chair and sat down. He said: "On account of Beth. I had to make her respect me before I could ask her again to marry me, so I figured I had a job to do."

Hoven took the star from his shirt and tossed it on the table. "Put it on. You're going to be the law in Bowstring County."

"I don't want it."

"Then you ain't the man I need," Hoven said bitterly.

"Take it," Beth said.

He picked up the star, wondering why she said that. Before he could support Beth, he had to reclaim his part interest in Broken Bell. He'd have trouble doing that and whipping the Knapps if he was bound by the obligations of a lawman.

"I know what you're up against, Tully," Hoven said. "Having the community behind you is one thing, but bucking the Knapps by yourself is something else. If Judge Carradine had backed me, I could have done the job, but he's no good, just no damned good."

"He's old . . . ," Beth began.

He faced her, his eyes hot with his anger. "Old or not, he's

81

no damn' good or he wouldn't be trying to make you marry Pete Knapp." He nodded at Tully. "Will you take the star?"

Tully looked at it, hating it and thinking that what he wanted to do could not be done if he took it, but for some reason he was not as positive as he had been. He said: "I'll see."

"Lytell and Quinn will be in the Casino tonight," Hoven said bitterly. "I ought to go over there and arrest 'em for beating me up, but I can't. That's why you've got to take the star."

"It'll just be in my way."

Hoven shook his head. "Might help you get some backing. I ain't sure anybody'll back you, but they might." He clenched his fists. "Quinn and Lytell could have killed me, but Rocky just wanted me shoved out on the scrap pile."

Tully rose and put the star in his pocket. He said: "A man's yellow as long as he thinks he is."

Hoven stared at Tully, the misery and bitterness that were in him showing in his face. He said dully: "That's right." He began to tremble, his self-control slipping from him.

Beth tugged at Tully's arm. "We'd better go."

Tully turned toward the door. Hoven jumped up and blew out the lamp. He said in a ragged voice: "Count the cost before you start wearing that star. You'll shoot Carradine or jail him before you're done. What will that do to you and Beth?"

"Depends on her," Tully said, and went out.

Beth followed, and, as they stepped off the porch, Tully heard Hoven shut and lock the door. They walked through the darkness toward the Carradine house. Before they reached it, Tully stopped and, putting his hands on Beth's arms, turned her to face him. He said: "He was right about the judge."

"Don't count the cost," she said. "Do what you have to do."

"I'm selfish as the devil," he said. "I'm just thinking about getting my half of Broken Bell back, and I've got to lick the Knapps to do that."

He kissed her, holding her hard in his arms as he felt the warm assurance of her lips, her body pressed against his. He wanted her as he had never wanted another woman, and he knew that she wanted him. There was no subterfuge about her, no denial of her hunger. When he let her go, he asked: "When will you marry me?"

"Tomorrow, if you want me."

"I want you all right. I'll see Mulcahy in the morning. He'll marry us no matter what the judge says. For a preacher Nat's got a lot of guts."

"Tully."

"If you're gonna change your mind. . . ."

"I'll never change my mind," she broke in. "It's about your saying that a man's yellow if he thinks he is. You shouldn't have said it."

"It's true. Bob knows he's yellow. He's trying to pass the star to me because he's afraid to do the job that's got to be done."

"You're still so sure of yourself," she said bitterly. "I was hoping that, when you got back, I'd find a little gentleness in you."

"I'm sure about Bob," he said, and walked away. He felt a vague stirring in his conscience, then it died. There had never been anything in his life to generate gentleness. He had no room for it now, not if he was to do Bob Hoven's job. Reaching Main Street, he turned toward the Casino.

IV

This was Saturday night, the one night in the week when Starbuck was crowded. It was early, but within another hour practically every rancher and cowhand in Bowstring Valley would be in the Casino with the probable exception of the Dorseys and Dave Lowrie who owned the Anchor 9.

Tully had reached the saloon when he noticed the big roan gelding and buckskin tied at the hitch rail. They were the

Dorseys' saddle horses, but it was incredible that either Ed or his boy Lon would be in Starbuck tonight. Ed used to say that a man who wanted a fight could always find one in town Saturday night, but a peaceable man had best stay home.

Tully swung toward the batwings, wondering if Ed had sold the horses, but, when he went in, he saw the Dorseys standing at the bar, their backs to him. He moved directly to them, saying: "Howdy, Ed."

Shocked by the familiar voice, Ed Dorsey swung around. Lon, too, had turned, and for an instant both stood motionlessly, staring at him. Then Ed said: "Tully." He held out his hand. "I'm glad to see you, boy, mighty glad."

Tully gripped his hand, feeling good about this. "I'm glad to be back, Ed." He offered his hand to Lon. "Howdy, Lon."

For a moment young Dorsey hesitated, then he said— "Broken Bell's busted, Tully."—and shook hands.

"Nothing to do but put a hole in Rocky Knapp's head," Ed said.

"And Pete's," Lon added.

This talk, coming from the Dorseys, was even less explainable than their presence here. Tully looked at Ed, and then at Lon. No change except that Ed's gray hair had turned completely white and Lon's face was thinner than it had been and one corner of his mouth twitched with irritating regularity.

"It can't be that bad," Tully said.

"It's worse," Lon said. "Well, we came to town to do something."

"To commit suicide," Ed added bitterly.

Others had recognized Tully and came up to shake hands, old Jake Furnes, the storekeeper, Doc Wallace, and other townsmen who had known Tully most of his life. The Box K bunch at the other end of the bar remained motionless, watching, the talk dying.

When Tully was alone with the Dorseys again, Ed motioned for another glass and, tilting the bottle, filled the three of them. He lifted his drink, saying grimly: "Here's to Hades, Tully."

"You mean for the Box K," Tully said.

"Yeah," Lon breathed, "that's better."

They drank and were silent for a time. Ed was a stocky man with a flowing white mustache and dark eyes. Tully had never seen him lose his temper, and even now he seemed very calm. Lon would look like his father in a few years. He had the same brown eyes, the wide nose, the square chin with a deep cleft. Steady, hard-working men, both of them. Now, looking at Lon, Tully sensed that he was keyed up. It wasn't like him.

"I saw Judge Carradine," Tully said finally.

"Then you know," Ed said. "Well, we're cleaned out. Nothing left to sell, so we won't be paying the judge off this fall."

"How'd they work it?"

"Dunno exactly except that they'd get 'em out on the lava where we couldn't track 'em. We figure they drove 'em north, butchered, and sold the beef to some shops in the mining camps. Now that Bob Hoven's gone, there ain't nobody to stop 'em."

Carradine's money had hired the new Box K hands, Tully thought. If so, it was a partnership. But what really hurt was that Carradine's influence, an intangible force but a strong one, was on the wrong side.

"When I left," Tully said, "I told you I didn't want no part of Broken Bell. I'd like to change my mind if I ain't too late."

"You never gave it up as far as I was concerned," Ed said. "I knew you'd be back on account of you're so much like your dad. Me 'n' Red made a pretty good team. He was always jumping into things and I was holding back. After he was killed. . . ." Ed paused, and then added bitterly: "Been nothing but holding back since. You hadn't growed up enough to do the jumping.

Maybe you have now."

Other men had drifted into the saloon, small ranchers and Dave Lowrie's Anchor 9 crew. Someone started a poker game at a back table and Matt Quinn and Carl Lytell sat in. Rocky Knapp moved along the bar to stand behind Tully. He said: "So you came back anyway." Tully wheeled, right hand instinctively dropping to gun butt. He waited, uncertain of Knapp's intentions.

Rocky Knapp was a small, knot-headed man with a hawk nose that gave his dark face a sort of pulled-out look. His eyes were beady black, and, when he smiled as he was doing now, his eyes were without humor. No one could read his face; his thoughts were secrets hidden in the shadowy recesses of a devious mind.

"What do you want, Rocky?" Tully asked.

"A talk." Knapp motioned to a table. "Let's have a drink."

Lon was watching, his body was tense as a tightly wound watch spring. He shouted: "Go to blazes! Tully belongs to Broken Bell."

"A man can't belong to something that don't exist," Knapp said.

Tully laid a hand on Lon's arm. "Slack off, boy. I'm curious."

Lon jerked free of Tully's grasp. "We're in town to have it out, Knapp. You've kicked us around till. . . ."

"Now, now," Knapp said easily. "All I want is to swap a little talk with Bain."

Tully swung away from the bar and walked across the room to the table. One of the Anchor 9 men called: "Hey, didn't know you were back, Tully! Where do you keep your scalps?"

"Inside my shirt, Slim. Don't see your boss."

Slim laughed. "You won't, either. Not here."

"Lowrie still playing a lone hand?"

Slim shrugged. "Dave allows there's no sense fighting for

men who won't fight for themselves. He don't come to town much."

"I'm going out to talk to him," Tully said. "You tell him."

"It's a waste of time, but I'll tell him."

Tully went on to the table and sat down, his back to the wall so he could watch Quinn and Lytell at the poker table and the other Box K men at the bar. Rocky joined him, carrying a bottle and two glasses.

"Got the best in the house." Knapp sat down. "Well, I've heard a lot about you, Bain. You know how grubline riders drift through the country, swapping gossip for a meal. You're quite a gunslinger, they say."

"I've been lucky."

"Takes guts to make luck."

It was not like Rocky Knapp to brag about an enemy. Tully said: "The same old Rocky, getting something the long way."

"This calls for slow and easy," Knapp said. "Been in town long enough to hear about Carradine and Hoven?"

"I've heard."

"Then you know we're big. With Carradine on our side we'll have the north half of the valley by the end of the year. Lowrie's out on a limb. A little more waiting and we'll have his Anchor 9."

"He's a tough boy, Rocky."

"Not too tough."

"Why didn't Quinn plug me today?"

"Changing the subject, eh?" Knapp filled the glasses and set one in front of Tully. "I'll tell you. I wanted to find out what you used for a backbone. You came on, so I figure you've got guts. I wasn't sure when you left. I'll hire you."

"I'm going back to Broken Bell."

"Oh, the devil, you're too smart for that."

"No, I'm just not bright. Not the way you figure." Tully

leaned forward. "I'm curious about another thing. How does it happen the Dorseys are still alive?"

"I don't waste lead on rabbits. It's the dangerous men who die. Men like you if they ain't on our side. Think it over."

"I'm done thinking."

Knapp tapped his fingers on the table top. "Look, Bain. The Box K has come a long way in three years, and the reason is I know how to use fear. It's a better weapon than a gun in your hand, if you handle it right. Now I've given it to you straight. You come over to us or we'll handle you like we done Hoven."

"Who did the job on Bob?"

"A couple of my boys."

Tully rose, sick of it. "Rocky, you're wasting your wind. I'm going to kill you. Not tonight, but I will."

"You're bucking a stacked deck!" Knapp turned in his chair, calling: "Pete, come here."

Pete Knapp had been standing at the bar. Now he came toward them, grinning, a gold tooth in the front of his mouth shining in the lamplight. He was a big man, as tall as Tully and wide of body with close-set blue eyes.

"Is he smart, Rocky?" Pete asked.

"No," the older Knapp said. "He aims to be a hero."

"Maybe for Beth Carradine." Pete tapped his barrel-like chest. "She's marrying me. Savvy?"

"You're sure as the devil wrong. I talked to her tonight."

Pete laughed. "You're the one who's wrong. Dunno that she'd be much of a wife, though, living by day beside Hoven and by night. . . ."

Tully jammed the table against Rocky, knocking him backward to the floor, whiskey from the bottle and glasses sloshing over him. Tully jumped at Pete, hitting him with a driving right that flattened his nose and brought a gush of blood from him.

Pete went back a step, surprised and hurt, then he let out a great bawl and swung at Tully. Tully ducked the blow, hearing a man in the back room call out: "Sit still, Quinn! You, too, Lytell." It was a familiar voice that Tully did not recognize at the moment.

Tully moved in close, battering Pete's face with rights and lefts. He took the big man's blows on his elbow and shoulders, constantly dodging and pivoting so that Pete could not get his hands on him.

Rocky had scrambled back to safety, and now he was screaming: "Bust him, Pete! Break his damned neck!" But Pete was a little drunk and he was slow, and Tully kept hammering him in the face with jolting blows that closed an eye and cut a lip and smashed his already flattened nose.

Pete began to give ground. Tully stalked him, a cold fighting machine. He kept pounding Pete's face with his left, rocking the man's head on his shoulders, then he had Pete backed against the mahogany. The big fellow braced himself against the bar and kicked out with his right leg. The boot caught Tully in the stomach and knocked him flat.

The crowd moved in to form a tight circle around them, the Box K men yelling for Pete to finish him, the others silent. Tully rolled and came to his feet as Pete lunged at him, a great fist swinging up from his knees in a powerful blow that would have knocked Tully cold if it had landed. Tully faded back, sucking breath into his lungs, and Pete charged after him, his face bloody.

The crowd gave way behind Tully. Pete grabbed a chair and threw it. Tully ducked and heard it crash against the wall behind him. He moved along the bar, slowly, backing away from Pete. He glimpsed a bottle on the mahogany and grabbed it, ducking as Pete threw another chair, then he moved in and smashed the bottle across Pete's head.

Pete toppled forward; he got his hands on Tully and held himself upright, his knees sagging. Tully tossed the neck of the bottle away; he brought his knee up into Pete's crotch, and Pete bellowed in agony. His grip relaxed, and Tully hammered him on his exposed chin, a short blow that knocked him cold.

V

Tully leaned against the bar, breathing hard, and again he heard the familiar voice: "Don't try it, Quinn." Tully wiped a hand across his sweaty face. The crowd had spilled away, and Tully, his eyes sweeping the room, saw that Lon Dorsey was standing by the batwings, ready to jump through them.

"Get some water!" Rocky was shouting. "Get this lard keg on his feet!"

Tully's gaze swung to the rear of the room. Bob Hoven stood there, a gun lined on Quinn and Lytell who were sitting at the poker table. Then his gun began to waver, and he pitched forward on his face.

Quinn and Lytell jumped up, hands moving to gun butts. Tully pulled his .44, calling: "Go ahead, Matt! You, too, Lytell, if you want to sleep in hell tonight."

They sat down again, hands placed on the table top.

Quinn said: "You're holding the fat ace, sonny, so I'll wait for another deal."

Tully nodded at Doc Wallace. "Bob was beaten up two weeks ago. Looks like he was hurt worse'n I figured. Tote him over to your office."

Wallace ran toward Hoven, Ed Dorsey and Jake Furnes a step behind him. They picked the sheriff up and carried him out of the saloon. Tully backed toward the batwings, still holding Quinn and Lytell under his gun. He said—"I'll be looking for another deal myself."—and then plunged through the batwings. He ran along the boardwalk to Doc Wallace's office and then, remembering the star in his pocket, took it out and pinned it on his shirt.

When Tully went into the medico's office, he saw that they had laid Hoven on the bed in the doctor's back room. Ed Dorsey asked anxiously: "Where's Lon?"

"Didn't see him," Tully answered. "How's Bob, Doc?"

Wallace stroked his goatee, frowning. "Looks like he's got a head injury. Concussion. If that's the case, it's hard to tell how bad off he is."

Ed was shaking Tully's arm. "Wasn't Lon in the saloon?"

"I didn't see him."

Ed swore and went past Tully in a lumbering walk. Furnes was staring at Tully, his faded eyes thoughtful. "You're tough, Tully, as tough as a boot heel."

"I need to be. When I left, Rocky Knapp wasn't so big. Now he's running things. What have you been doing, you and Doc and everybody else?"

"No need to hooraw us," Furnes said angrily. "Easy for you to come back and start talking. Wasn't easy to keep it from happening."

Tully walked to the bed and looked down at Hoven's pale face. This was a hell of a thing, he thought. He had misjudged Hoven and he was ashamed. He asked: "Ain't there anything you can do, Doc?"

"Keep him in bed," Wallace said. "That's all."

The shame grew in Tully as he stood there. Hoven had asked for help and he hadn't understood. He said: "Bob's been in his house ever since they beat him up. Beth's been taking care of him. Reckon she was the only person he figured he could trust."

"The hell." Furnes was indignant. "He could have trusted any of us, me or Doc or the preacher."

"Ever do anything to make him think that?"

Furnes shook his fist at Tully, shouting: "Stick around and

the Knapps will take some of your toughness out of you! Then you won't talk so big."

Tully pointed to the star. "See that?"

"You think one man can . . . ?"

"Looks like it'll be one man." Tully turned to the medico. "How do you figure the judge, Doc?"

Wallace spread his hands in a gesture of helplessness. "You can't look inside a man and tell what's there, Tully. I don't know. I just don't know."

"What are you fixing to do, Tully?" Furnes asked.

"Go to bed." He nodded at Hoven. "Rocky won't let Bob get on his feet if he can help it."

"I've got a shotgun and I'll sleep on the couch," Wallace said.

Tully swung toward the front door and turned back when Furnes said: "Tully, I asked you what you were going to do?"

"I'm going out to Broken Bell in the morning. Maybe everybody else around here is licked, but I ain't."

"You're gonna need help. I was thinking of Dave Lowrie."

"I know Dave," Wallace said. "Forget it."

"Well then, get a posse," Furnes insisted. "Go after the Knapps and string 'em up."

"You ain't so old you can't fork a horse," Tully said. "Will you ride with a posse?" When Furnes hesitated, Tully added— "That's what I thought."—and walked out.

Tully got his war sack from the livery stable and crossed the street to the hotel. Horses were still racked in front of the Casino, but the roan and buckskin that belonged to the Dorseys were gone. They'd lit a shuck out of town, he thought. All their tough talk hadn't amounted to a damn.

As soon as Tully closed the door of his hotel room, he shoved a chair under the knob, wondering what the Knapps and Judge Carradine would do. He tugged off his boots and, unbuckling his gun belt, put his Colt under his pillow. He lay down on the bed, his mind working on the puzzle of Carradine's change. Rocky had said he'd used fear. Maybe that was the answer.

Tully had barely dropped off to sleep when a shot sounded from down the street. Horses thundered past the hotel, and a moment later Matt Quinn bawled: "We'll get 'em, Rocky!" More horses pounded along the street. Tully went back to sleep, thinking it was no concern of his, probably just a drunken brawl.

It seemed only a moment later when someone pounded on his door. Still groggy from sleep, he called: "Who is it?"

"Beth. You've got to come with me, Tully."

He was fully awake then. He jerked the chair away from the door and opened it. "What happened?"

Beth came into the room. The moonlight that spilled through the window fell across her slender body; he saw that her hair hung down her back and that she had slipped a robe over her nightgown.

"Lon Dorsey shot and killed Pete Knapp tonight," she said.

He didn't believe it. Maybe the judge had gone out and heard some crazy rumor. Tully said: "Nothing I can do. Go on back to bed."

"Tully, you've got to come with me," she said in a frantic voice. "Ed's talking to Dad now. He wants to sell Broken Bell."

VI

For a long moment Tully stood motionlessly, staring at Beth. He had no doubt now that what she was saying was true, and still he found it incredible.

"Lon didn't have it in him," Tully said finally. "He just wasn't man enough."

"Ed wouldn't lie about a thing like that," Beth said. "I heard him say Lon had been set on coming to town tonight and having it out with the Knapps. He said it had been working on Lon until he'd gone crazy."

Tully struck a match and would have lighted the lamp if Beth had not caught his arm and blown the flame out. "Rocky's still in town," she said. "He might be watching your window."

"Might be at that," Tully muttered, and, sitting down on the bed, pulled his boots on.

Rocky Knapp had loved Pete with as much feeling as he was capable of having for anyone. He was the older of the two; he was smarter than Pete and he had always looked out for him. Now it was probable that Rocky was out of his head, prowling the streets with a gun in his hand, and it was possible he'd think Lon had circled back to town and had sought refuge in Tully's hotel room.

Buckling his gun belt around him, Tully picked up his .44 from the bed and slipped it into his holster. He walked to the window and looked down into the street. A full moon had rolled up into the sky, but the dust strip below him was dark with shadow and he could not make out anything that looked like a man. If Rocky Knapp was there, he was probably hiding in the alley opening across the street, his eyes on the window of Tully's room or the front door of the hotel.

"How'd you get in?" Tully asked.

"I came up the back stairs and went down to the lobby to get your room number. The clerk said Rocky and one of his boys, a kid named Billy Dawes, had been in about an hour ago to look at the register."

The Dorseys had ridden out of town ahead of Quinn and most of the Box K crew. Lon would not have come back to town. Tully knew him too well to think he would. Considering it now, it seemed to Tully that Rocky Knapp must have known that, too. If he had come into the lobby with one of his men to find out the number of Tully's room, they were gunning for Tully, not Lon.

"Come on," Beth said impatiently. "Ed won't stay there long."

"No sense walking into a slug," Tully said.

He drew his gun and, dropping his Stetson over the barrel, eased it through the door. A wall lamp near the head of the stairs threw its murky light along the hall. When there was no sound, Tully said—"Stay behind me."—and, putting his Stetson on his head, moved swiftly through the door, and stood with his back to the wall. There was no sound except the snoring of some drunken cowhand in a room down the hall.

Tully waited there a full minute, left hand holding Beth against the doorjamb at his side. She whispered: "You didn't used to be like this, Tully. You didn't have an ounce of caution in your body."

"I've got a little more'n an ounce now," he said, "mostly because I figure I've got something to live for."

He ran along the hall to the back stairs, floorboards squealing under his feet. His mind was on Rocky Knapp, trying to guess what the man would do, now that he knew Bob Hoven was up and active. Only one thing was certain. Knapp would kill Tully, if he could, because he considered him dangerous. He was close to achieving what he wanted, so close that Pete's death would not change anything. He could not afford to let Tully's return stiffen the resistance that he had spent three years breaking down.

Tully reached the bottom of the stairs and stopped, again holding Beth behind him. He said: "If Rocky was watching from across the street, he probably saw you in the lobby and he'll figure out why you came."

"He couldn't know Ed was in our house," she whispered. "Ed left his horse at the edge of town and he crawled most of the way to our back door."

"But he'll guess who you came for," Tully said. "I'm going out. If he's here, or got one of his men in the alley, I'll soon know. You wait till I get fifty feet away, then you come running if nothing's happened."

Gun palmed, Tully slipped into the alley. Shadows were deep here, covering Tully unless a Box K man was within a few feet of the back door of the hotel. Tully had a sudden dislike for the whole business. The same shadows that hid him would hide an enemy.

A pile of cans and boxes that had been thrown out by the hotel cook lay within a few feet of the back door. Stooping, Tully picked up a can and tossed it across the alley. It banged against the wall of a building with startling loudness and caromed off into the darkness. A gun opened up at once, three twinkling ribbons of flame that lanced out of the darkness. Tully answered the shots, running toward the man and keeping close to the wall. This wouldn't be Rocky, he thought. The man was too tricky and too careful.

Tully stopped, hunkering against the hotel wall. He was not far from the man, but for a moment he could hear nothing. He could not tell whether he had hit the fellow or not. Then he caught the rasping sound of a dying man laboring for breath. Tully crawled along the alley, afraid that Beth had followed him.

He reached the man's body. The fellow was sprawled out, flat on his back. His breathing had stopped, and, when Tully picked up a wrist, he could find no trace of a pulse. He lit a match, cupping the tiny flame with his left hand. He'd got the man above the stomach, blood a dark, spreading stain on his shirt front. He called—"Beth."—remembering that he had seen this fellow in the saloon. He was young, hardly more than a kid.

Tully straightened up, waiting for Beth, and he thought of the three years he had spent, taking fighting wages from men like Rocky Knapp. Crazy, he thought bitterly, a damned fool to fight for someone else when he didn't care how the thing went, risking his life while the man who had hired him stayed in the background. Lives came cheap to men like that. Knapp wouldn't give a thought to the kid's death. He'd hire another man and forget this one.

Beth was beside Tully then. He said: "Reckon Rocky's on the other side of the hotel, but he might come back here to find out what happened."

They ran across a vacant lot toward the Carradine house, the moonlight around them, but no shot came racketing out of the alley shadows. Rocky Knapp had not been in a hurry to find out who had gone down in the exchange of shots.

Beth asked: "Who was it?"

"Stranger. Not more'n a kid. I saw him in the Casino tonight with the rest of the Box K outfit."

"Billy Dawes, the one who I told you came into the lobby to look at the register," Beth said bitterly. "Wanted to be tough like Matt Quinn and Carl Lytell."

They reached the Carradine yard and went on up the path. Tully thought that he'd been lucky and wondering what decided matters of life and death. They'd bury Billy Dawes in Starbuck's boothill, they'd put a marker, and weeds would grow on the mound of earth. Maybe he had a family somewhere who would never know.

Well, it had been different with Tully. He'd had no family, but Beth would have cared. Then he put the somber thoughts out of his mind. He'd changed the day he'd received Bob Hoven's garbled letter, changed so much that he'd never be a rootless drifter again with a gun for hire. Or maybe he hadn't changed until he'd got here and found out that Beth still loved him.

He followed Beth along the dark hall to Judge Carradine's study in the rear of the house. She opened the door and went in, saying: "Tully's here."

Carradine was dressed. He swung around, swearing as he peered through his steel-rimmed glasses. He said: "Get out, Beth, get out and take this. . . ."

"Shut up, Judge." Tully went into the room and closed the door. "I just killed a man. You hear the shots?"

Ed Dorsey sat on a black leather couch, thoroughly scared, his red-rimmed eyes showing he had been crying. It startled Tully, for he had known Ed as a gentle, mild-mannered man who had never permitted his emotions to get out of control.

Ed started to get up, but his knees would not hold him. He dropped back, whispering: "Was it Rocky?"

"I wish it was," Tully said. "I wish to hell it was. No, he was just a kid. Beth said his name's Billy Dawes. Tried to get me when I came out of the back of the hotel." He pinned his gray eyes on Carradine. "I reckon you'd like it better if it had gone the other way."

Carradine sat down at his desk. "Yes," he said. "Everything was going all right till you came back, everything. Now it's all snarled up."

Tully crossed the room and sat down beside Ed. Beth remained standing by the door. She said: "I heard Ed come in, and I listened long enough to hear what he wanted, then I went after Tully. He owns half of Broken Bell. Remember, Dad?"

Carradine sat motionlessly, his claw-like hands gripping the arms of his swivel chair, his yellow-skinned face an expressionless mask. "I can't understand what's got into you, Beth. I've done everything I could for you. Now you're doing all you can to defeat me." He motioned to Tully. "When you bring a killer like him into the house, you bring nothing but trouble."

"A killer," Beth said with cold contempt. "Are you so wise you can judge between one killer and another?"

Ed Dorsey whispered: "It'll be daylight before long. I've got to get out of town before then. Lon's waiting for me. You know what will happen if they catch us."

"I'll pay you a thousand dollars," Carradine said, "if you'll get Bain to sign over his half of Broken Bell."

"He can't do that," Tully said. "I came back to live on Broken Bell."

"They'll kill you," Carradine said harshly. "You can't go out there. Don't you understand, Bain? Pete's death doesn't change anything. It'll just make Rocky worse."

For the first time Ed Dorsey saw the star on Tully's shirt. He pointed to it, his finger trembling. "Why are you wearing that?"

"I'm Bob's deputy."

"Lon murdered Pete," Ed said tonelessly. "Shot him in the back from the batwings. I suppose you'll fetch him in."

"I wish you hadn't told me." Tully stared at the floor, knowing he would have heard sooner or later anyhow. He knew what Hoven would do and what Hoven would expect him to do. "It puts the law on Knapp's side."

"If you hadn't come back, I'd have talked Lon out of it," Ed asserted. "He's always been afraid to fight. You know that. You used to rawhide him about it, then after we got cleaned out, Lon went kind of crazy. Kept saying you'd have stopped 'em if you'd been here. When he saw you lick Pete tonight, he said he was gonna finish it. He walked the streets for a while. I moved the horses and tried to get him to leave town, but he wouldn't go. Finally he went back to the Casino, but he didn't have the guts it took to face Pete. He just plugged him and ran."

Now, looking at Ed Dorsey's face, pale and taut and filled with misery, Tully sensed the despair that was in the man. He said: "All right, Ed, blame me if it'll make you feel any better. You want some money to get out of the country. That it?"

"Yeah, that's it." Ed licked dry lips. "Come fall, Carradine will get the outfit anyway. I just wanted him to give me enough to get a start somewhere else, and he'd have title to the place without waiting."

Tully took a wallet from his pocket and counted out $500. "That's all I can spare, Ed. I can't arrest Lon, if I can't find him. Anyway, you ain't selling Broken Bell no matter what happens. It's mine now, but, if you ever come back, you'll have your half."

Ed took the money, the corners of his mouth quivering. He said in a low tone: "I ain't really blaming you, Tully. I made Lon like he is. I'm the same way, but you was different from the first, just like your dad was different from me." He rose, staring at Carradine. "I hope there's a purgatory, Carradine. There must be for men like you, pretending to be so good when you're rotten all the way through."

Ed Dorsey went out, Beth shutting the door behind him. When his steps died, she said coldly: "I'm marrying Tully, Dad. Today. What are you going to do about it?"

"Nothing. It's too late now. I . . . I. . . ." He shook his head. "Everything I've done was for you."

Tully rose and looked down at Carradine. "I figure Quinn and Lytell beat Bob up two weeks ago. He's in Doc Wallace's office now, unconscious."

"I took his supper to him after you left," Beth said, "but he was gone. What happened?"

Tully told her, then asked Carradine: "If Bob gets so he can talk, I'm hoping he can identify 'em. I aim to throw 'em in the jug. What sort of a trial would you give 'em?"

"A fair trial," Carradine said, "but the chances are you won't get a conviction."

"That's what I figured," Tully said. "Why don't you get under a rock with the rest of the crawling things?"

Carradine turned to look at Beth. "You're still going to marry him after hearing that?"

She nodded. "I love him. That's all the reason I need." She swallowed. "You've been a stranger to me for months. Sometimes I wonder if I ever knew you."

"Nobody did," Tully said. "That's what I can't savvy. Have

you changed, Judge, or did no one ever know what you really are?"

Carradine rose and began walking around the room. He stopped and stared at the fireplace; he raised his eyes to the shelves of law books that covered one side of the room. He said: "Go upstairs, Beth."

Tully nodded at her. "Pack what you've got to have. I'm taking you out of here."

"We'll go out to Broken Bell," Beth suggested. "What we have to do we'll do together."

"No," Tully said. "You can stay with the preacher. We've got to wait a little while."

She opened her mouth, wanting to argue, then she whirled and ran out of the room, saying nothing. Tully said: "Are you proud, Judge, now that Beth knows what you are?"

"She doesn't know. She'll never know all of it, I hope." Carradine shoved his long, skinny hands into his pants' pockets. "You asked me if I'd changed. No, I was always this way, wanting more power and money than I had, and I knew I was too slow getting it."

"But damn it," Tully protested, "people respected you. Now you've thrown it away."

"Are you sure people respected me?" Carradine faced him, smiling slightly. "Anyhow, you can't buy anything with respect, Bain. You're talking like a child. This is a rough country. Those who can will take and the sheep like Ed Dorsey will lose. That's the way it is." The smile left his lips. "I wanted a deed to Broken Bell. If you hadn't walked in here, I'd have got it. Now I'll get it from you."

"I don't think so."

Carradine nodded. "I'll get it, some way, and I'll get the Box K. This country needs a dam and that's the place for it, up there above your buildings. I need both sides of the creek." He sat down at his desk again, bony hands knotted. "A while ago you asked me if I was proud. I've lived in this valley a long time, thinking and dreaming and looking ahead. I'm a visionary, but I'm practical, too. If I had another ten years, I'd change this country so you'd never know it. No, I'm not proud because I haven't got ten years."

"You'd change it," Tully said, "for your profit. That it?"

"A man's a fool to work for anyone's profit but his own," Carradine said.

"I think you're lying."

Carradine's yellow-skinned face was stirred by curiosity. He asked: "Why do you think that?"

"I made one mistake tonight. Bob lied to me when he let me think he was afraid. He was hurt, but I didn't know it. When the chips were down, he backed me up and saved my life. I'm wondering if I'm making the same mistake about you."

"No," Carradine said. "I quit pretending when I lined up with Rocky Knapp. Time was running out on me, and I was tired of pretending."

"Something else," Tully said. "Rocky figured he could buy my gun. He should have known better. I'm wondering why Matt Quinn didn't plug me when he had a chance this afternoon. You knew I was coming back and you told Rocky. He had Quinn waiting for me this side of Stone Saddle."

"Rocky figures anybody can be bought," Carradine said. "So do I when I have the right price to offer a man, but Rocky isn't smart enough to consider a fine point like that. It's always money with him, and he thought he had plenty to hire your gun. Then Beth would get over the notion she's in love with you. She's pretty idealistic, you know."

Tully nodded, thinking that this was the way Rocky Knapp's devious mind would work. He said: "Rocky told me that fear was as good a weapon as a gun and he's used it on you. What were you afraid of?"

Carradine laughed. "Rocky thinks he's smart, but he really isn't. He talks about the dam like it was his notion all the time, but I thought of it ten years before he did. As far as weapons are concerned, greed is a good one and that's what I used on him."

"You still ain't told me what you're afraid of."

"Nothing," Carradine snapped, "except losing Beth and my investment here in the valley."

"So you were the brains all the time," Tully said bitterly.

"Sure. No sense lying. Beth won't believe you if you tell her. After you left, Rocky took over the south half of the valley, all but the Anchor 9. Meanwhile he's had to borrow from me. That's his mistake. When you get down to cases, Bain, money is a better weapon than either fear or greed."

Now, looking at Carradine's thin, sick face, Tully had no doubt that the man was being honest with him. Tully said: "I don't savvy. You're painting yourself pretty damned black."

"And you're wondering why." Carradine scratched the tip of his long nose, studying Tully's face with calculated intentness. "I'll tell you, Bain. Two reasons. First, Beth is the only person in this world I love and I'm hoping you're smart enough to see what I'm offering you on account of her. Second reason is that I need a fighting man and you'll do. I'm done with Rocky."

"You think you have the right price to buy my gun?"

"I think I have." Carradine held up two fingers. "Beth." He lowered one finger. "An empire, the biggest cattle empire in the Northwest, given time to develop it. You have both time and money, or you will have."

"You hold a mortgage on the Box K?"

Carradine nodded. "That's why I'm done with Rocky. They've pulled in some money from the beef they've rustled, but Rocky's had a big payroll to meet, so he kept borrowing from me. Men like Quinn and Lytell come high." Carradine tapped the desk top with bony fingers. "Interested?"

For a moment Tully considered Carradine's offer, and he could not help being tempted by it. A cattle empire just as Carradine had said, handed to him on a silver platter. No two-bit, bankrupt spread stripped of cattle, its mortgage due in a few months. Then the moment passed and he shook his head.

"No deal," he said, and turned to the door.

"Wait." When Tully swung back, Carradine said: "Remember one thing. I love Beth. I won't give her up to you or any man. I won't lose her."

"You've already lost her."

Carradine bowed his head. "For the moment, but I'll get her back. Until then it's up to you to keep her safe. I suppose I can stand losing her for a time, but I couldn't stand it if anything happened to her."

"She'll be safer with me than she ever was with you," Tully said, and left the room.

He shut the door and waited in the hall until Beth came down the stairs from her room, a valise in her hand. She had put on a brown suit; her hair was brushed and pinned in a bun on the back of her head. The sun was up, and, when he opened the front door and the early morning sunlight fell upon her face, he saw that she had been crying.

"Are you sure this is what you want?" Tully asked.

"I'm sure."

"It doesn't look like I've got much chance to save Broken Bell. Where'll we be then?"

"It'll be all right, Tully. I know it will."

He took the valise. "It's got to be. I love you so much it's got to be."

"I can't help thinking what these three years have done to you and Dad," she said with more bitterness than he had ever heard in her voice before. "People used to say you'd turn out bad, and now you're back and you're fine and good, and Dad. . . ."

"He's what he is," Tully said somberly, thinking that he was probably the only man in Bowstring County who knew exactly what Judge Carradine was. "We can't change him, Beth. We'll have to make our life without him."

"We will," she said quickly. "I'm sure we will."

VII

Nat Mulcahy was a big, red-faced Irishman who had preached in Starbuck as long as Tully could remember. He taught school during the winter, and, when the weather warmed in the spring, he rode all over Bowstring County, calling on ranchers who lived too far from town to come to church. When there was sickness, he was often ahead of Doc Wallace, and in the fall, if help was scarce, he made a hand at roundup. He was welcome in every home in the county, even those in which the man of the family was a professed atheist.

Tully had gone to school with Mulcahy and on occasion had been whipped by him. He had heard Mulcahy preach at his father's funeral, and, although he had been a boy at the time, he had remembered it, for Mulcahy had not tried to save the souls of the living. He had given a high tribute to a brave man whose most grievous error had been a slow draw.

Now, as Tully knocked on the preacher's door, he heard a baby crying in the back of the house and he wondered if he was making a mistake. The Mulcahys had ten children in a house that was half big enough for them. When the door opened, Nat Mulcahy took one look at Tully and let out a whoop, a grin crinkling his red face.

"It's Tully Bain!" the preacher shouted, and shook hands. "Heard you were back." His face was suddenly grave as he glanced at Beth, sensing that something was wrong. "How are you, Beth?"

"We want to get married," Beth said.

"Well, it's sure early in the morning for a wedding, but I guess it's not too early."

"Not today," Tully said. "Beth can't stay at home. I know you're crowded, but I was wondering if you could take her in."

"Why, Tully, we're not crowded at all," Mulcahy said. "We've got lots of room. Of course we'll take her in."

"Then I'll be sloping along. . . ."

"Let me go with you." Beth gripped his arms. "I can't stand it here, not knowing what's happening."

"No," Tully said, "I'm going alone, but when I get back, you be ready with the marrying, Nat."

"I'll be ready," Mulcahy said. "Come on in, Beth. Breakfast is ready."

Still Beth hesitated, her hazel eyes on Tully, and he sensed the worry that was in her. He said: "Don't you fret none about me. I'll be back."

"I know you'll be back," she said. "It . . . it couldn't be any other way now."

She put a hand on his arm, squeezing it, her lips sweetly set, her eyes telling him she loved him, then she turned and, picking up her valise, went into the house. Mulcahy said—"Wait a minute, Tully, I want to talk to you."—but followed Beth.

Tully waited impatiently, wondering what the preacher wanted. The crying of the baby stopped. Tully grinned, remembering that Beth had a way with kids and she'd be welcome because she would make herself useful.

In a moment Mulcahy returned, his sun-reddened face touched by good humor. He said: "You've got the best woman in Bowstring County outside Missus Mulcahy. Say, why don't you have breakfast with us, Tully?"

"I've got to slope along," Tully said. "I ain't sure what's got hold of me, Nat, but seems like I can't wait to get to Broken Bell."

"Your horse in the livery stable?" When Tully nodded, the preacher said: "I'll walk a piece with you."

They turned toward Main Street, Tully sensing there was something on the preacher's mind. He was usually an outspoken man, but now he glanced at Tully, frowning, indecision gripping him. Then he said: "I know what happened last night. I'm glad to see that star on your shirt. Things would have been different if you'd got back two weeks ago and Bob could have had your help."

"I came as soon as I got his letter. Guess I wanted to come all the time, but didn't figure I'd be welcome."

"I know what the talk was about you," Mulcahy said impatiently. "It's possible Carradine started it because he didn't want you to marry Beth. You made it easy, having a talent for getting into trouble, but I never subscribed to the notion you'd turn out bad. Bob Hoven said a dozen times in my hearing that all you needed was time. I figured that was right. Well, you've had it."

"Yeah, I've had it," Tully said somberly, "and now I'm back, but I don't like the shape things are in."

"Most of us don't. Doc told me what you said last night about him and Furnes. You're right. We let it happen. We just sat around and let it happen, and I guess I'm to blame more than anyone."

"How do you figure that?"

"I knew Carradine," Mulcahy said. "I've always wanted to believe good of a man. A weakness of mine, I suppose. Anyhow, I leaned over backward hoping he had changed, but now it looks like the devil's got him." He paused, the turmoil of his thoughts arousing an uncertainty in him. "But the Scripture says not to judge. Maybe I'm wrong saying the devil's got him. How can you be sure?"

They had reached Main Street, deserted at this early hour. Tully stopped, staring at the preacher and finding no answer to his question. He said: "Let's have the rest of it."

Mulcahy leaned against the wall of the Mercantile, staring westward toward the line of mountains where Bowstring Creek was born. He said slowly: "I'll tell you, Tully, because you're marrying Beth and you ought to know. She's not Carradine's daughter."

Startled, Tully asked: "You sure?"

Mulcahy nodded. "I knew Carradine in Dodge City a good many years ago. It was an accident that brought me here. I mean, I didn't purposely follow him. I had no reason to. I just drifted farther West with my family, and, when I got here, I stayed, knowing that Starbuck needed a preacher."

When Mulcahy stopped, Tully said impatiently: "Well?"

"It's been a hard decision," the preacher went on. "I mean, about whether to tell what I knew or not. When I got here, he had a good reputation and I tried to keep from judging him. Like I said, I wanted to think he really had changed."

Mulcahy brought his gaze to Tully's face. "The only man in the valley who has never been in my church is Carradine. Even Dave Lowrie and the Knapps have come once in a while. I'm going out to the Box K to preach Pete's funeral right after the service this morning. I'm not looking forward to it, but I'll have to go."

"Tell Rocky I'm at Broken Bell."

"I'll tell him if you want me to," Mulcahy said, "although it will only make trouble for you. But what I was going to say is that Carradine was a crooked, jackleg lawyer who got run out of Dodge City because of a confidence game that he put over. His wife was a good woman, and Beth was her child by a former marriage. Carradine took Beth with him, and, after I got here, he seemed to love her and to be doing a good job raising her. Now I wonder if he hasn't used her to get a hold on the Knapps."

"Then he missed out," Tully said. "Pete's dead."

Mulcahy spread his hands. "Who knows? There's still Rocky, and I've seen him look at Beth the way a man like that looks at a woman. That's one reason I hope you'll marry her right away." He hesitated, then added: "I thought you should know, Tully. You may have trouble with Carradine."

"I'll handle him," Tully said.

"As a preacher I'm supposed to avoid violence," Mulcahy said, "but by nature I'm a violent man. It's the heaviest cross I've had to bear. I'd take a gun and settle all this if I followed my natural inclination, but, when I pray about it, I know it's the devil talking to me and not the Lord. Yet, when I think about what has happened in this valley, I'm not sure. Five murders. I've preached at the funerals of those men. I've done all I could for the widows before they left the valley. I don't know. Perhaps violence is the only way to bring justice to this country."

"Carradine says he won't live long."

"He may be dying," Mulcahy admitted. "He's failed just the last few months. But that doesn't answer my problem. Sometimes I think I haven't done my duty by failing to tell what he used to be."

Staring at the preacher's craggy face, Tully sensed the deep misery that was in the man. It surprised him, for if there was a man in the valley who should have a clear conscience, it was Nat Mulcahy. But he had his problem in the same way Bob Hoven had had his. Neither was a free man. Mulcahy was tied by his religious convictions, Hoven by his obligation as a lawman.

"It seems like Carradine has made himself pretty clear lately," Tully said.

"He's come into the open," Mulcahy agreed. "He's refused to extend the loans he's made and he has given Bob Hoven no co-operation at all, so Bob has been pretty helpless. By fall, Carradine will own almost all of the valley north of the creek if he closes the ranchers out. Except for Dave Lowrie's Anchor 9, Rocky Knapp controls the south half of the valley." He made a weary gesture. "But whether my telling about Carradine's past would have made anything different is something I don't know."

"We'll see about what's ahead," Tully said. "No use worrying about what's behind."

"I know," Mulcahy said. "That's the way to look at it. Well, don't worry about Beth." He scratched a cheek, troubled eyes on Tully. "It's a long trail back once you let things get out of hand the way we've done, but the spark of liberty or independence or whatever you want to call it is never dead. Just fan it into flame, Tully, but be careful while you're doing it."

"I'll be hard to catch," Tully said, and walked away.

He stopped at Doc Wallace's office and went in. The medico bounced out of his back room when he heard the door open, shotgun on the ready, then he paused, grinning sheepishly.

" 'Morning, Tully." Wallace lowered the shotgun. "I'm a little boogery. Shouldn't worry, though. Rocky Knapp left town with Pete's body an hour or so ago."

"How's Bob?"

"He came out of it all right. I've just got to keep him quiet." The doctor pulled at his goatee, eyes narrowing thoughtfully. "I've got Billy Dawes laid out yonder." He jerked a hand toward a door to his right. "They found him in the alley back of the hotel."

"I shot him," Tully said, and told the doctor what had happened. "I'm going out to Broken Bell now, but I was wondering if I could see Bob before I go."

Wallace hesitated. "I don't want him worked into a lather. . . ."

"I'll be careful."

"All right. Don't take more'n a minute."

Tully nodded, and walked past the doctor into the back room. Hoven lay on his back, his face pale. Tully pulled a chair to the side of the bed and sat down. He asked: "How do you feel?"

"Fine," Bob answered. "That fool medico thinks he's gonna keep me here till Christmas, but he's crazier'n a loon. I'm getting up pretty soon."

"You stay there. I've got the star where it belongs." He tapped his shirt front. "Right here."

Hoven grinned and turned his head to look at Tully. "I knew you'd put it there."

"I came to apologize." Tully swallowed, finding this harder to say than he had thought it would be. "You tried to make me think you were yellow. Hell, I should have known you were just putting on. Reckon I ain't much of a friend, mistrusting you. I'm sorry I said what I did."

"Forget it. I thought it was the only way I could make you mad enough to take the star. Reckon it was."

"No, it was your coming into the Casino. You saved my hide." Tully swallowed again. "I'm beholden to you. . . ."

"Shut that up," Hoven said wearily, and closed his eyes. "I got you into it, so it was up to me to be on hand when the ruckus started. I didn't want to, but I had to do it. Reckon I was foolish not to call Doc, but I didn't trust nobody except Beth. Thought I was safer if nobody knew."

Tully rose. "I sure don't know what to do about Carradine, but I'll handle Rocky."

"And Pete. He ain't gonna forget the licking you gave him right away."

Tully had not realized until then that Hoven hadn't heard about Lon Dorsey murdering Pete Knapp. Panic momentarily crowded into Tully as he considered it. If Hoven knew, he'd want Tully to start after Lon, but that was one thing he could not do.

"Yeah, I'll watch out," Tully said. "Now you stay here where you belong."

"Sure, right here on my back," Hoven said bitterly. "Devil of a place to run a sheriff's office from."

"That's what you got a deputy for," Tully said, and left the room.

Doc Wallace followed Tully into the street and closed the door. He said: "Hell's gonna pop now. Rocky thought a lot of Pete. If he don't catch Lon, he'll take it out on you."

"He tried to last night." Tully rolled a smoke, thinking of Dave Lowrie who had always puzzled him, a lonely man who had never neighbored with anyone and seldom came to town except when he needed supplies. "How well do you know Dave Lowrie, Doc?"

"Furnes shouldn't have mentioned him last night. Well, I suppose I know him as well as anybody outside of his own crew. Pulled a tooth for him once. Hurt like sin but he never let out a yip."

"What are you trying to say?"

"Nothing, except that I don't know him and nobody else does. Unfriendly cuss. Furnes knows as well as I do that Dave Lowrie is the last man in the valley who'd burn any powder helping another man."

"It's to his interest to keep Carradine and Rocky from taking the valley over."

"Think he'd see that?" Wallace shook his head. "No, sir, Dave allows he'll ride his horse and it's up to you to ride yours. Don't count on any help from him."

"He's got the biggest spread south of the creek," Tully said doggedly. "Used to have a crew of four men. Still got 'em?"

Wallace nodded. "Likewise he still doesn't throw in with his neighbors at roundup time. Doesn't use the mountains for summer range. Keeps his herd down to what he can run right here in the valley."

"I'm gonna see him anyway," Tully said, and turned away.

"Wait." When Tully swung back, the doctor said: "I keep thinking about what you said last night after we brought Bob over here. About the Knapps running things and you asking us what we'd been doing."

"Shouldn't have said it," Tully muttered. "Should have stayed here myself."

Wallace shook his head. "No, you were too young then. Now you know what to do. Trouble is, every time I add you up, I just get one man."

"There's you and Jake Furnes and the preacher. A few others. Like Jeff in the livery stable."

"Poor stuff for fighting, Tully. What are you going to do?"

"Ride out to Broken Bell and see what Rocky does."

"What are you trying to do, make bullet bait out of yourself?"

"That's about it," Tully said, and went on to the hotel, leaving the medico staring bleakly after him.

VIII

Tully got his war sack from his room, ate a quick breakfast, and within the hour was riding out of town, headed west. The air was still and cold; the sky was clear, although clouds still hugged the mountain crest to the north.

The road paralleled Bowstring Creek, a deep, slow-moving stream at this point with willows crowding its banks. He passed ranch houses, smoke rising from their chimneys. The outfits close to town were piddling, ten-cow spreads, the owners in debt to Carradine and too poor to hire more hands and buy bigger herds.

Haystacks had diminished until there was feed for only a few more days at best. As the miles fell behind, Tully saw that Matt Quinn had been right when he'd said the spring was late and the grass slow to start. The next few weeks would be tough.

The country lifted when Tully was a few miles west of town, a piney ridge that angled southward directly ahead of him. He could hear the creek to his left now. From here on westward to its source it was a clear, swift-running stream. When the hot weather came and the snow began to melt, it would be a brawling torrent, running up to the banks until it slacked off in midsummer to become so small that a man could jump across it.

Bowstring Valley was like many other cattle ranges Tully had seen since he'd left. A dam on beyond Broken Bell would save the early summer run-off and guarantee a steady flow. The land along the creek could be flooded and the little ranchers would be able to raise enough hay to make it through the winter without the yearly worry about grass that plagued them now.

Ordinarily development took money, and no one in the valley had money but Judge Carradine. Thinking about what Carradine had said early that morning, it occurred to Tully that this was what the man had in mind, a cattle empire with the point of control up here beyond Broken Bell, the one logical dam site in the country.

Again Tully's mind turned to Dave Lowrie who believed that a man could live alone. But Lowrie, like everyone else in the valley, never had enough hay to get through the winter. It was, Tully thought, the one approach that could be made to the man. Once Carradine and Knapp were smashed, the valley ranchers, by pooling their labor, could build a dam without Carradine's capital if they were content not to hurry it. Then

Tully realized ruefully that it was wishful thinking, that time held the answer, and, as things stood, there was no time.

The country tilted more sharply now, Tully beginning to climb the first shoulder of the spur that made the western boundary of the valley. The land on both sides of the creek still held the gray, drab hue of winter, with here and there a wind-shaped juniper dotting the sage-covered, sandy soil. Presently he reached a fork in the road, one branch swinging south across the creek to Knapp's Box K, the other, faint wheel tracks that showed little travel, going on upstream to Broken Bell.

Tully wondered where the Dorseys were now. Lon, he knew, would be plagued by the hell of his conscience. Ed, too, for he blamed himself along with Tully for what had happened. Resentment stirred in Tully. Ed had no reason to blame him for Lon's weakness. Lon had been a coward when he was a boy. As a man, he was still a coward, and, if the self-abasing knowledge of his cowardice had made him shoot Pete Knapp in the back, it was his fault and none of Tully's.

He reached a barren streak in the road, the dirt still soft from a recent rain, and he was suddenly aware that a rider had come this way not long before. He reined up and stepped down. Stopping beside the tracks, he examined them carefully. Just one horse, headed west. Tully judged that the tracks had been made only a few minutes ago.

He rose, eyes raking the pines that were directly ahead of him. Broken Bell was not more than half a mile from here. Most of the Box K crew, probably all of them except Billy Dawes who was dead, had gone after Lon. Rocky, then, must be the one who had traveled the Broken Bell road, possibly thinking that the Dorseys had returned to their home. Or, and this seemed more likely, Rocky had guessed that Tully would do exactly what he was doing. Now Rocky was somewhere ahead, hiding behind a pine or a boulder, waiting for Tully to ride by.

Caution made Tully swing upslope to his right, listening for any unnatural sound, his eyes seeking hiding places where Rocky could be waiting for him. The pines were scattered here, the slope covered by alternate patches of shadow and sunlight. He reached the ridge top and turned west along the crest, the Broken Bell buildings visible to him now.

He followed the ridge until he was directly above the buildings. There was no sign of life below him, no movement of any kind, but he had not expected any. If Rocky Knapp was here, he would leave no obvious indication of his presence. Still, Tully had not foreseen that Broken Bell would appear as completely deserted as it was.

Depressed, Tully sat his saddle for a long time, looking down at the ranch where he had grown up. The square log house, the barn and sheds, the pole corrals, the fenced plot of ground just above the house where his father was buried. Even considering the manner in which he had left, Tully had not thought his homecoming would be like this.

A queer, undefined uneasiness began working through him. Homecoming wasn't the word. This deserted, bankrupt ranch was no home at all. Not even a horse in the corral. Almost every head of stock gone, Ed Dorsey had said. Carradine with a mortgage that couldn't possibly be paid off by the due date this fall.

Boy-like, he had permitted himself the luxury of an impossible dream that had excluded the Dorseys. At odd moments, when he'd had time to picture things as he'd like to have had them, he had thought of Broken Bell as his outfit.

Good Hereford stock had been part of the dream, fine horses, a bunkhouse big enough for a fair-size crew. Invariably Beth had been a part of it, Beth who would be waiting for him when he rode in at dusk. Consciously he had assured himself he'd never come back, but still there had been this dream of owner-

116

ship that had lingered tenaciously in the back of his mind.

Now, thinking of the few dollars left in his pocket, he thought how utterly impossible it was. Sure, Beth would marry him and move up here and they could starve together, providing he could get Judge Carradine off his neck and lock Rocky Knapp and his crew up in jail where they belonged. It was just a crazy, kid dream without substance, without the slightest chance of making it come to life.

He rode down the slope, the old rashness crowding him. If Rocky Knapp was here, Tully would take his chances with him. The man wasn't a gunfighter, and neither Matt Quinn nor Carl Lytell would be with him. Tully passed his father's grave, noticed that Ed had kept it scrupulously clean.

It struck Tully that it was strange the way people had made a legend out of Red Bain, yet they had perversely looked down upon Tully because he was so much like his father. Now they had changed their feelings about him, Furnes and Doc Wallace, and probably the rest of them. They needed him, they were pinning their hopes on him, thinking that by some miracle he would turn out to be the man their imagination had made out of Red Bain.

Tully had no illusions about his father, although he had always been proud of him. Probably Ed Dorsey had been right in saying that Red Bain had been too proddy, too hot-tempered, a good man with his fists but not particularly fast with a gun, and that they'd made a good team, Ed holding Red back but with Red giving the partnership the drive it needed. Ed had never said it in just those words, but Tully knew that was what he'd thought.

Well, they could spin their campfire yarns about Red Bain; they could expect Tully to be another Bill Hickok as they liked to think his father had been. But he wasn't. He knew his limitations. Any way he looked at it, the odds were too long to be

licked, and that made him a fool for being up here. As Doc
Wallace had said, no matter how many times he counted Tully
up, he was still one man.

But fool or not, he was here and he'd see it through. He rode
slowly, hand on gun butt, and, as he came around the barn, he
saw two things that made him pull his black to a stop. A faint
trace of smoke showed above the chimney, and there was a
horse ground-anchored in front of the house. He had been too
far away to see the smoke that was wiped out by the wind the
instant it rose above the chimney, and the horse stood directly
in front of the house so that it had been hidden from him.

The wind, quite strong now, tugged at his hat and he raised a
hand to pull it down on his head. It wasn't Rocky Knapp who
was here. He wouldn't have left his horse in front of the house
and he wouldn't have built a fire. It wasn't the Dorseys, either.
The horse was a small bay gelding he had not seen before.

Tully sat motionlessly, puzzling over this, uncertain whether
to ride on to the house or rein back out of sight. Then the front
door swung open and Beth came out on the porch, the wind
beating at her and molding her dress against her small, trim
body. She motioned to him, shouting something that was lost in
the wind.

For a moment Tully remained there at the corner of the barn,
an involuntary sigh of relief breaking out of him. Then he rode
on across the yard, suddenly angry with her. He had left her
where she would be safe. She had no business coming out here.

"How'd you get out here ahead of me?" he demanded.

She tossed her head defiantly. "I was riding while you were
gabbing. Put the horses up and come in and cut me some wood.
I've picked up every chip I could find."

"I told you to stay at the preacher's. . . ."

"I know what you told me," she said tartly, "but that didn't make me stay. Now do what I told you. I've got dinner almost ready."

He stared at her, sensing the futility of argument. She was here, a fact that he had to accept for the moment. Later he would find some way to persuade her to go back to town. He said—"All right."—and, taking the bay's reins, he led him back to the barn.

He watered the horses at the log trough, taking a drink from the pipe that brought water from a spring above the house; he stripped gear from the horses and, finding some oats in the barn, fed them. He walked to the woodpile, the wind striking him squarely in the back. It took only a moment to split an armful of wood; he carried it into the house, and dropped it into the box behind the range.

Beth pounced on it and filled the firebox. "Isn't very dry," she complained. "Must have rained harder here than it did in town." She handed him the water bucket. "Make yourself useful."

"Beth, you can't. . . ."

"I can and I am. Go on now. We won't eat for a while. The fire got too low. I tried to cut some wood, but those blocks were too big."

He went back into the wind, not wanting to argue with her. Ed Dorsey used to say that women were handy for cooking, but they complicated a man's life. As Tully waited for the bucket to fill from the pipe, he decided that Ed had never made a more truthful statement in his life. He returned to the house and set the bucket on the stand beside the back door.

"Beth, you can't stay. . . ."

"Get washed," she said. "The fire picked up faster than I thought it would."

He poured water into the tin basin, washed, and, finding a comb stuck between two logs above the washstand, ran it through his hair. He and the Dorseys had used that comb for years. Irrelevantly he noticed that most of the teeth were gone. He tossed the water out through the door and set the basin back on the stand.

"We might as well have this out," he said hotly. "I wanted to keep you out of this."

She whirled from the stove to face him. "Did you expect me to stay in town when you came out here to get shot?"

"I sure did. I wouldn't have taken you to Mulcahy's if. . . ."

"Tully Bain, I wouldn't give two shakes for a woman who hid behind her husband. I've seen too many who were like that. I just won't be that kind of a wife."

Her hazel eyes were bright with anger; it had set fire to her cheeks. She was uncommonly pretty, he thought, standing there by the stove, her shoulders back, her high breasts rising and falling with her breathing.

"Reckon I ought to be proud of you," he said.

"You ought to be," she flared. "If you want a limp rag for a wife, you'd better start looking for another woman."

"I am proud of you," he said, "but we ain't married, and I don't want to start with folks talking about us."

"I'm not afraid of talk," she insisted. "I'm not afraid of anything but losing you. What's more, we'd be married right now if you had an ounce of gumption in you."

She flounced around, and, picking up a fork, began to poke at the meat. She said in a low tone: "I thought that was what we were going to the preacher's for this morning."

He came up to her and put his arms around her. "I don't want you hurt. About dark I'll have my hands full, if I'm guessing right."

"And I don't want you to get what Bob got." She was stiff in his arms. "I know what you're up to. You told Mulcahy to tell

Rocky you'd be here. You're just trying to make bait out of yourself."

He dropped his arms. "I didn't know what to do. Toting a star is something new for me, but I figured that, if Rocky came after me and I plugged him, some of our troubles would be over."

"All by yourself," she said scornfully. "You must think you're a man and team with a dog under the wagon."

"If I hadn't taken the star. . . ."

"That's got nothing to do with it. You'd be out here anyway. I don't care how big a reputation you made for yourself when you were gone. It won't cut any ice with Rocky Knapp." She turned to look at him. "In case you didn't know, I can shoot a gun as straight as any man. I found Ed's Winchester and he's got plenty of shells. Now go sit down. This meat's done."

He pulled a chair back from the table and sat down, running a hand across the oilcloth surface. The kitchen was exactly as he remembered. Ed had done the housework, leaving the riding the last few years to Tully and Lon. He had left the house as immaculate as ever, even though he must have known that he'd never be back. Ed Dorsey had his own peculiar brand of pride.

Beth had found a pot of beans in the pantry that she had warmed up. She had baked biscuits, made coffee, and fried meat; she set the food on the table and began to eat, ignoring Tully. He looked at her, unable to say anything for a moment as he realized how much he loved her and how great the danger was that she was insisting on facing with him.

Still he did not want to quarrel with her. He said carefully: "Why didn't you stay at Mulcahy's?"

"For one thing, they're so crowded that one of the kids would have slept on the floor." She glanced up, cheeks still rosy with the anger that was slowly dying in her. "But that wasn't the real reason. Can't you understand, Tully? I had to be with you. I'd rather die than lose you again." She swallowed and lowered her gaze. "I guess I'm just spooky, but I can't get rid of a feeling that something's going to happen that will keep us apart."

He said—"Won't be no trouble till evening, I reckon."—and began to eat.

IX

When dinner was over, Tully got up and walked through the house, stirred by boyhood memories. The three years he had been gone had seemed an eternity, but now that he was back, he was astonished how perfectly everything in the house fitted the picture that his memory had retained.

The pot-bellied heater in the front room. The homemade couch with the Navajo blanket thrown over it. Ed had bought the blanket from a transient peddler years ago. The rocking chair that Ed had made. The bookcase filled with Lon's books. The rough pine table in the middle of the room, a few papers and dog-eared catalogs cluttering its top.

The Dorseys had used the back bedroom. Tully stepped into it, but he did not linger there, for it seemed to him the room was still filled with their presence, Ed with his gentle voice, and Lon, cringing with the fear that had been born in him.

Tully felt a little guilty because he had always been impatient with Lon, but now he had some notion of the battle that young Dorsey must have fought with himself before he had found the courage to ride into town last night. But it had been a poor kind of courage that had finally brought him to the place where he had shot a man in the back, even when that man was Pete Knapp.

There was no justice to it, Tully thought as he went into his bedroom. Lon had been a good hand with cattle. Under different circumstances they could have been happy here, the three of them. Or four, if Tully had brought Beth to live with the

Dorseys. They had always liked her and she had liked them.

For a long time Tully stood in the middle of his room. The Dorseys had left it just as it had been when Tully had ridden out except that Ed had made the bed. Probably no one had slept in it since. Tully's fishing pole leaning against the wall. Some pine cones he had taken a fancy to when he was a kid. A handful of colored rocks. Antlers belonging to the first buck he'd shot.

Tully wheeled out of the room, unable to stand it any longer. He had lost all concept of time, and, when he went back into the living room, he saw Beth was sitting in the rocking chair, her hands folded on her lap, the chair squeaking as she rocked.

She said: "It's cold, Tully. Why don't you build a fire in the heater?"

He nodded and went outside, returning a moment later with some pitchy kindling. He got the fire going, and, because there was nothing else to do and he could not shake off the galling sense of uneasiness, he went back to the chopping block and split enough wood to last a week, venting his feelings with vicious, downward swings of the double-bitted axe. He filled the wood box in the kitchen, brought a couple of chunks into the living room, and dropped them into the pot-bellied heater.

Beth, still sitting in the rocking chair, said: "Not much to eat in the pantry, Tully. I guess Furnes had cut off their credit."

"Blamed tight-fisted son," Tully said, and thought of the few dollars in his pocket. But Furnes wanted something done about Rocky Knapp. He'd make a deal.

Beth rose and came to him. She gripped the front of his coat, turning it back with her hands as she lifted her face to his. She said: "Tully, it's got to be this way."

He shook his head. "No."

She swallowed. "I'd rather have been married at home, a big cake and a reception and all, but I guess it's got to be this way, just you and me."

He looked down at her, not knowing what to say and realizing that his return had brought this whole thing into sharp
focus. Courage was something he had always admired in anyone
and this girl had it, so much that it made him ashamed. He was
afraid. It was in his belly like a cold rock and there was no use
to deny its presence. He had never been a man to underestimate
his enemy. The chance he had of beating Knapp's bunch added
up to slightly more than zero. And he still didn't know how to
get Beth out of here.

"Sure, you and me and the preacher."

She tugged at his coat. "Tully, Tully," she breathed. "We could
be happy if we had a chance."

"We'll make our chance," he said.

She turned from him and walked to a window. He saw her
stiffen, heard her breathe: "Come here, Tully."

He crossed to her. Three riders had broken out of the timber
on the other side of the creek and now they forded the stream,
hoofs driving the water upward and to both sides in long, silver
ribbons, the wind whipping the spray downstream. One was
Mulcahy, one Rocky Knapp, and for a moment Tully could not
identify the third who had dropped behind. Then they came up
the bank and Tully saw that it was Judge Carradine.

Beth whirled away from Tully. She took a rifle down from
pegs on the wall and jacked a shell into the chamber. She said:
"I'm not going back to town with them, Tully. Make that clear."

He nodded, and, lifting his gun from leather, checked it, and
slipped it back. He watched them pull up in front of the house
and step down, Knapp's dark, hawk-nosed face sullen and filled
with smoldering fury.

They crossed the porch to the door and Mulcahy knocked.
Tully opened the door. He said evenly: "Come in, Nat."

"I asked Rocky and the judge to come here," Mulcahy said.

"I have something to say that has a bearing on all of this."

Knapp pinned beady eyes on Tully's face. "I ain't here to visit, Bain. I'll say what I have to say and get out."

Carradine seemed oblivious to everything except his weariness. He stepped back to the edge of the porch and gripped a post, his thin body sagging. "I'd like to sit down, Bain," he said, his voice so low that Tully barely heard him.

"All right," Tully said, and stepped aside.

Mulcahy went in first, then Knapp. Carradine was the last, Tully closing the door behind him. When he turned, he saw that Carradine had stopped as if frozen, staring at Beth, his breathing an audible sound in the sudden silence.

"So it wasn't enough for you to leave my house," Carradine said. "You've got to come out here and move in with him and live like a. . . ."

"Carradine," Tully said, "you claim you're a sick man, but, sick or not, I ain't above beating hell out of you if you say what you're fixing to."

"And I won't stop him," Beth said tonelessly.

Carradine stumbled across the room and dropped into the rocking chair, his mournful face more yellow than ever. He licked liver-brown lips, dark eyes fixed on Beth. He said dully: "I came here because the preacher asked me to. I thought we could work something out, but it looks like there's no use to try."

"There's my way," Rocky Knapp said confidently. "Bain, last night I gave you a chance to get on the right side and you turned it down." He nodded at Beth, standing motionlessly with Ed Dorsey's cocked rifle in her hands. "Put that up."

Mulcahy went to the stove and stood with his back to it. He said: "Put it up, Beth. I'm going to do the talking."

She glanced at Tully and he nodded. Reluctantly she eased the hammer down and leaned the rifle against the wall. "All right, talk," she said. "Talk all you want to, Nat. You, too, Knapp, but before you start, I can tell you that you're done stealing. We're going to make this country too hot to hold you."

He laughed. "I reckon not." He nodded at Tully. "From what the judge tells me, Broken Bell is yours. You paid Ed Dorsey for his share last night."

Tully nodded. "We didn't sign anything, though."

"No need to, not with the judge being in the position he is. I went easy with the Dorseys because I wanted a clear title. Just moving onto their range wasn't enough, not when you want to build a dam like we do, so I figure the best way is to just buy you out fair and square. How much do you want, Bain?"

"Funny you want to buy, Rocky," Tully murmured. "Last night all you wanted to do was to murder me."

"Last night I couldn't think of nothing but Pete," Knapp said, "and, since the Dorseys wasn't around, I figured you was next best. Anyhow, today I'm looking ahead. Well, I guess maybe it would be worth some cash money to get you out of the country."

Probably the Dorseys had had a chance to sell, Tully thought, and they had turned it down, so Knapp had gone ahead, breaking them slowly in the belief that sooner or later they would sell and give him the clear title he wanted.

"No," Tully said. "You're afraid, Rocky."

"Of what?" Knapp snorted.

"Me. Quinn tried to shove me back over Stone Saddle and missed. You tried to hire my gun and missed. Pete tried to kick hell out of me and missed. Your Billy Dawes tried to kill me and he's dead. So you decided you'd better buy me out, and that makes me a pretty big man." Tully shook his head. "We ain't selling."

"We?" Knapp asked.

"Me 'n' Beth. We're gonna live here. I turned my back on

126

Broken Bell once, but I'll never do it again."

"So you're gonna live here," Knapp jeered. "In debt and on a stripped range. You're licked and I think you're smart enough to know it."

"Get out," Beth commanded. "All of you. Nat, I'm surprised at you, coming in here . . . with. . . ."

"Wait," the preacher said. "I haven't started my talking yet."

Carradine sat quietly, bony hands clasping his knees as he rocked gently. He asked in a low tone: "What will it get you to tell, Mulcahy?"

"What the hell is this?" Knapp demanded.

"You're tied in with a crook, Rocky," the preacher said, "a bigger crook than you are. Carradine's a jackleg lawyer who got run out of Dodge City years ago and came here, pretending he was a pillar of the law."

"Shut up," Carradine breathed. "I'm telling you, preacher. Shut up."

Bewildered, Knapp looked at the lawyer. "So the preacher knew you before. Small world, they say. Reckon it is."

"Too small for Carradine," Mulcahy said dryly. "I've kept still, not sure what good it would do to tell what I know and not wanting to hurt Beth. Besides, there was always a chance that Carradine might have turned over a new leaf like he pretended. I know better now. The Lord takes His vengeance, Rocky, like I said when we buried Pete."

"I heard you say that," Knapp said angrily. "I didn't like it. The Lord ain't big enough to do you and Bain any good. You won't leave this house alive. I just decided."

"Don't ever count the Lord out," Mulcahy said evenly. He turned to Beth, his red, Irish face troubled. "I'm sorry that I have to tell you this, but it's best that you know. Carradine is not your father."

"He's lying!" Carradine screamed. "You never had any reason

127

to think I wasn't your father. Haven't I always treated you like my daughter?"

Tully, watching her, saw that she was not as shocked by what Mulcahy had said as he'd thought she would be. Then it struck him that she had suspected the truth. It was probably the reason she had been willing to leave the house that morning.

"No," she said in a low voice. "You didn't treat me like a daughter when you wanted me to marry Pete Knapp. I think I must have known then."

"That's beside the point right now," Mulcahy went on. "You're rid of him and you'll marry Tully and that's the way it ought to be. Rocky's the one who'll get hurt." He gave Knapp a straight, severe stare. "Without the judge's legal shenanigans, you haven't got the slightest chance to secure a legal title to Broken Bell."

"Then I'll get along without it!" Knapp shouted. "I've had all the bad luck I can stand, losing Pete and Billy Dawes last night. I've burned some powder and I'm willing to burn some more to get what I want."

"Murder has its limitations when you don't have a friend in the judge's chair." Mulcahy turned back to Beth. "I'm going to do something I should have done before. I have no excuse for not doing it except that I was afraid the same as everybody else has been afraid."

Mulcahy licked his dry lips, his gaze touching Tully's face briefly, and Tully saw that the preacher was still afraid. For the first time Tully realized the full significance of what Rocky Knapp had said the evening before in the Casino, that he had learned to use fear and it was a stronger weapon than a gun. But now for some reason Nat Mulcahy had found an inner strength that enabled him to rise above his fear.

"Funny thing," Tully said. "We've all been afraid of Rocky, I reckon. Even the judge, although I suppose he won't admit it now. Well, Rocky ain't much to be afraid of. If we got rid of Quinn and Lytell, Rocky would be the scaredest man in the valley."

"But you ain't got rid of Quinn and Lytell," Knapp said complacently. "Well, I'm getting out of here. I've had my say and you turned me down. No reason for me to stay."

"You take a step toward that door and you'd better go for your iron," Tully said, "because I'll be putting a slug through your brisket. You're going to jail."

"On what charge?" Knapp demanded.

"Murder will do till something better comes along," Tully snapped. "Like rustling."

"Wait," Mulcahy said. "I'm not done. You're right about us being afraid. Remember there have been five murders in the valley since you left and that's enough to make anybody afraid. We've all wondered who would be next. But it came to me while we were burying Pete that it was better to be dead than to live in fear. I think that is a discovery the judge has never made."

"He never will," Knapp said scornfully. "We'll keep on working together like we've been doing."

"No." Mulcahy shook his head. "You're finished, Rocky. You're nothing without the judge's money and his court."

"I've still got 'em," Knapp said. "You're wasting a lot of words, preacher."

"I have often wondered where Carradine got his money," Mulcahy went on, ignoring Knapp. "He may have stolen it, but I've got a hunch I'm going to work on, and, if I'm right, Carradine doesn't have a nickel to his name."

Carradine was on his feet, trembling, his yellow face marked by splotches of dull red. He asked thickly: "What is your hunch, preacher?"

"I'm going to get in touch with the Dodge City authorities," Mulcahy said. "You were married while I was there, and I remember that shortly after that you bought a house and started acting like a rich man. Beth's mother died about that time. We'll find out her maiden name and we'll trace where she came from. I'm thinking we'll find out she was a wealthy woman and that you've been using her money which rightfully belongs to Beth."

Carradine swayed on his feet. He began to curse, his right hand moving inside his coat. Tully drew his gun, saying: "Don't try it, Judge."

Beth had snatched up the rifle and was holding it on Knapp. She said: "Let's get back to town. Knapp should have been in jail a long time ago."

But Rocky Knapp was unconcerned. He had turned to the window, a triumphant grin tugging at the corners of his mouth. He said: "You won't be taking me anywhere, Bain."

Tully wheeled to the window. The Box K crew was fording the creek, Matt Quinn and Carl Lytell riding in front.

X

This was the moment Tully had been afraid would come, the Box K crew outside and Beth still here in the house, but the one thing he had not counted on was having Rocky Knapp under his gun. That fact, if used properly, might determine the difference between life and death for all of them.

Tully swung back to Carradine who had started to reach for his gun again, hesitantly, in the manner of a man who had never placed his trust in guns. "Keep your gun on Knapp, Beth," Tully said. "Judge, lay your iron on the table."

Carradine peered at Tully through his steel-rimmed glasses, still uncertain of himself. His glance wavered toward Beth and came back to Tully. Then he obeyed, laying his short-barreled .38 on the table and stepping back. The Box K men had reined up outside, Quinn calling: "Rocky!"

Knapp started toward the door and stopped when Tully said:

"Stand pat, Rocky." He jerked his head at Beth. "Keep the judge covered. He might get some crazy notion."

Tully's gun was on Knapp. Beth gave Tully a questioning look, but he told her nothing. Slowly she made a half turn so that her rifle was on Carradine. This was not the way Tully wanted it, but he had no choice. He could only hope that Beth would do what she had to do if Carradine lost his head and tried to get his gun from the table or rush Tully.

"I'm surprised at you, Rocky," Tully said. "You outsmarted yourself."

"You mean I outsmarted you," Knapp said. "That's what you're surprised at."

"I reckon you figured we'd let you walk out of here or maybe you never counted on Beth being handy with a Winchester. Anyhow, you're licked and you're going to jail."

Knapp shrugged, beady eyes probing Tully for a sign of weakness. He shook his head. "You can't get out of here."

Again Quinn called—"Rocky!"—impatiently this time.

"Open the door and send 'em home," Tully ordered. "If you reach for your gun or call 'em in, I'll plug you."

"In the back," Knapp said scornfully. "Like that Dorsey pup got Pete."

"Maybe I will," Tully snapped. "Get rid of 'em."

Still Knapp stood motionlessly, eyes pinned on Tully's bleak face. He must have convinced himself that Tully would do exactly what he said. He swung toward the door and opened it. "It's all right, Matt. I don't need you. Take the boys back to the ranch."

Tully stood close to the wall, watching Knapp. From where he stood he could not see the men outside, but Mulcahy had moved to the window. He said: "Quinn figures something's wrong."

"Make it sound good, Rocky," Tully breathed.

131

"What the devil you waiting for?" Knapp shouted. "Go on back, I told you!"

"This don't smell good!" Quinn yelled. "Why ain't you coming back with us?"

"I'm trying to make a deal with Bain," Knapp answered. "I tell you to go on back. Dunno why I have to give an order three times."

"If Bain is trying to run a sandy on us," Quinn bellowed, "I'll get him! Tell him that!"

"Sure, sure," Rocky said and, stepping back, slammed the door, his hawk-nosed face heavy with sullen anger. "Satisfied?"

"I will be if they vamoose," Tully said. "What are they doing, Nat?"

"Pulling out," Mulcahy said, "but we're not out of the woods yet."

"Neither's Rocky," Tully said. "Didn't figure on it working out quite this way, did you?"

"Go to hell," Knapp muttered.

Tully grinned at him, a taunting grin designed to make Knapp go for his gun in a sudden flare of rage, but Rocky Knapp was a patient man when his life was in the balance. Tully was not sure why Knapp had come in with Mulcahy and Carradine, then it struck Tully that the answer might be quite simple. He had been so successful using fear as a weapon that it had probably never occurred to him Tully might reverse the situation.

There was this long moment of silence, then Mulcahy said: "They're gone."

"Saddle Beth's and my horses and fetch 'em to the back door," Tully said. "Then get the three in front and take 'em around to the back. We'll go up the ridge."

Mulcahy hesitated, then nodded, and left the house. It took a moment for Tully, his mind focused on Rocky Knapp, to realize why the preacher had hesitated. There was a possibility that

Quinn and the rest of the Box K crew might have pulled up in the fringe of timber and were waiting to cut down anyone who left the house. It had been a mistake to send Mulcahy for the horses and Tully regretted it at once. He opened the door and called—"Come back, Nat!"—still holding Knapp under his gun.

Puzzled, the preacher swung around and plodded back to the house. He came in, asking: "Can't you make up your mind?"

"I finally did," Tully said. "Rocky, pull your gun and lay it on the table beside Carradine's. Make it slow. I'd rather take you back dead than alive."

Rocky obeyed, his sullen anger leaving his face. He seemed quite unconcerned as he moved from the table to stand beside Carradine. He said: "You can't make this stick, Bain. The judge will have me out of the jug by noon tomorrow. Hoven never had any evidence against me. How do you think you'll find any?"

"I ain't real particular," Tully said. "Right now all I want is to slap you into the calaboose, and I ain't no stickler for evidence like Bob was. Nat, take the guns. Put Carradine's in your waistband and keep your fist on Knapp's. I'll get the horses."

"That ain't your meat, is it, preacher?" Knapp asked maliciously.

"I can't turn back now that I've gone this far," Mulcahy said. "It has occurred to me that I may be the tool the Lord is using to exact His vengeance. I will kill you if you get out of line."

"You wondering about Matt and Lytell being back with the boys?" Knapp asked, nodding at Tully. "They went after the Dorsey pup, you know."

"Yeah, I was wondering about that," Tully admitted.

"They finished the chore," Knapp said. "They got young Dorsey in the back just like he got Pete. That's the way we take care of anybody who gets in our way."

Tully wheeled out of the room, not certain whether Knapp was lying about Lon Dorsey or not. He glanced at the bank of timber on the other side of the creek, seeing nothing that indicated the Box K men were there, and walked rapidly to the barn, straining the impulse to run. A sense of imminent danger knotted his belly muscles and brought an odd prickle to his skin. Five men had been dry-gulched in Bowstring Valley in the last few months; he might be the sixth. Then he was in the barn and some of the tension left him.

He saddled both horses and led them to the back of the house, then got the three that were in front and led them to where the others stood. Still no rifles cracked from the timber, no sound at all to break the mountain silence. Quinn, Tully decided, must have obeyed Knapp's orders and taken the Box K crew back to the ranch.

Tully opened the back door and called: "Let's ride!"

They came at once, Carradine walking as if he were in a daze, Knapp with his shoulders back, beady eyes filled with defiance. Beth and Mulcahy followed, Beth carrying Ed Dorsey's Winchester, the preacher holding Knapp's Colt. He had slid Carradine's gun inside his waistband as Tully had directed.

Mulcahy was the last out of the house. He pulled the door shut, eyes turning to Tully. He said: "It's no wonder so many people can't determine the difference between right and wrong when a man like me has difficulty who has spent most of his lifetime seeking divine guidance on every decision he makes."

Carradine's head snapped up. "Yet you would condemn me. Who are you to judge . . . ?"

"No one," Mulcahy broke in. "That's why I have remained silent as long as I have. I couldn't look into your soul."

"Then why did you . . . ?"

"Five men have died in this valley," Mulcahy said. "Without you Knapp would be nothing."

"There have been extenuating circumstances," Carradine broke in.

"That would excuse murder?" Mulcahy shook his head. "I think not. I would have spoken up a long time ago if I had thought it would do any good. Now that Tully. . . ."

"Oh, shut up. If I'm going to jail, let's ride." Knapp gave Tully a thin smile. "I'll feel safer there than with this locoed preacher riding behind me with a six-shooter."

But Carradine was not ready to go. He stood beside his horse, one hand on the horn, his thin, yellow face touched by an inner feeling Tully had never seen there before.

"Wait, Bain," Carradine said. "I was wrong a while ago to think about using my gun. I want to set some things right. The money rightly belongs to Beth just like you guessed, preacher."

"Damn it . . . !" Knapp shouted.

"Shut your mouth," Tully said. "Go ahead, Judge."

"I loved your mother, Beth." Carradine shivered as a cold blast drove down the creek. "I love you, and, although you may not believe it, I have consistently tried to do what was best for you. Now everything's different. Pete's dead and Bain isn't the crazy kid he used to be."

"Did we come out here in the cold to talk?" Knapp yelled. "Let's start . . . !"

"Rocky, I won't tell you again to shut up," Tully said. "Say your piece, Judge."

Carradine's bony knuckles were white on the saddle horn. He leaned against his horse, his dark eyes on Beth as if so hungry for the sight of her he could not satisfy himself.

"I've used your money wisely, Beth," Carradine said. "There's enough gold in the safe to restock Broken Bell. All the mortgages are there. You'll own the Box K before the year's out, and everybody will be better off when you do."

Tully, watching Carradine closely, had a feeling that the man

135

thought he was dying. Knapp shifted his weight uneasily, glancing at Tully, and for the first time his knobby face seemed to lose its expression of cool detachment. Beth took a step toward Carradine and stopped, caught in a trap of conflicting emotion. Only Mulcahy seemed entirely at peace, satisfied with the turn things were taking.

"Remember I've been kind to you and I've loved you, Beth," Carradine said. "I could have taken your mother's money and left you alone in Dodge City." He brought his eyes to Tully. "If I'm able, we'll have a hearing for Rocky in the morning."

He turned and put a foot in the stirrup; he lifted himself into the saddle with a great effort and slumped over the horn, holding himself upright by sheer power of will. Knapp yelled—"Hold a hearing for me, will you?"—and lunged at Carradine, but he was too far from him. Tully got between them and, grabbing Knapp by the shoulders, shook him.

"Get into the saddle," Tully said ominously. "I'm riding behind you. If Quinn starts a ruckus, you'll get it first."

Knapp stared at Tully, his face black with smoldering fury. "We'll see," he muttered. "You're still holding the aces, but we'll see."

Tully released his grip, and Knapp mounted. Mulcahy said in a low tone: "Carradine is not able to ride."

"He's got to. We can't stay here." Tully mounted his black. "We're going up the ridge, and, when we get to the top, we'll swing east. I think Quinn went back to the Box K, but if he didn't, it'll take some tall shooting from where he is to tag us."

They started up the slope, Knapp leading, Tully riding directly behind him, his gun held in front of him. The others strung out behind, Carradine still slumped forward. They reached the top, paused a moment to blow their horses, and then turned toward town. Tully, his eyes sweeping the valley below him, could not catch any hint of movement in the pines beyond the creek.

The chill wind beat at their backs, the sun giving little heat to the valley that still held the drab, gray look of winter. They were in the open now, angling toward the road, and, when they reached it, Mulcahy brought his horse to a faster pace and came up beside Tully.

"I think Carradine's dying," the preacher said. "We can't keep on."

"What do you want us to do?" Tully demanded. "Stop and let Quinn and his bunch move in on us?"

"There are a few ranchers along here," Mulcahy said. "Somebody would take Carradine in."

Tully shook his head, giving the preacher a sour look. "Getting righteous all of a sudden doesn't change what he is, Nat. Anyhow, it's my guess he's got a trick up his sleeve."

"I don't think so. He's got to the end of his twine and he knows it."

"You're still trying to spot some good in him. In some ways you ain't very smart, Nat. Even a preacher can't see what ain't there."

Mulcahy gave up and dropped back to ride beside Carradine. The sun sank below the western rim and dusk moved out across the valley in steadily thickening layers of purple shadow. Then the lights of Starbuck were ahead of them.

Beth appeared at Tully's side, asking: "What are you going to do?"

"Lock Knapp up."

"We're taking Dad home. I mean the judge. I guess I'll always think of him as Dad." She took a long breath. "Tully, I can't leave him now. You don't forget all a man has done for you, I mean, at a time like this, when he hasn't got long to live."

Beth was the kind who wouldn't, Tully thought, but he said nothing. He could never trust the man again, and he doubted that Carradine was as bad off as he pretended to be. More than that, he was convinced that the man had been completely dishonest in what he had said back at Broken Bell.

"Is it all right for me to go with him?" Beth asked. "I . . . I owe it to him. You don't care?"

"You do what you have to do," Tully said. "I ain't one to tell you."

She reached out and gripped his arm. "It won't be long, Tully."

He said—"Sure."—in a troubled voice, convinced that Carradine had said what he had in order to work on her sympathy.

Beth reined around and rode back to Carradine and Mulcahy. They took a side street to the Carradine house and Tully and Knapp went on to the jail. They dismounted and went in, Knapp standing aside as Tully opened the heavy door into the cell that made up the rear half of the building.

"When I don't show up at Box K, Matt will be here," Knapp said. "You know what will happen to you then?"

He was worried now. It showed in his voice, in the deep frown that creased his forehead, in the uncertainty of manner that was not like him.

"You're still trying to scare me, Rocky," Tully said. "I'll fetch some grub as soon as I put the horses up."

Knapp stepped into the cell and Tully closed the door and locked it. He put the key into his pocket and, going back into the street, mounted the black and, leading Knapp's horse, rode into the livery stable.

The hostler had seen them come into town. He stood inside the archway, and, as Tully stepped down, the old man said: "You done a day's work today. I never figured I'd live long enough to see Rocky Knapp in jail."

"The job is to keep him there, Jeff," Tully said.

He walked rapidly to the hotel dining room, and ordered a

meal for Knapp. He did not have any idea how much time he had. Sooner or later Quinn and his men would come, and he still had no help. Because he had to have someone, he strode around the store to the back room where Furnes slept and cooked his meals.

"You're spending the night with me in the jail," he told the storekeeper. "You wanted something done. All right, it's done. I've got Rocky Knapp in jail, and I figure I'll need some help to keep him."

Furnes stared at Tully, unable to believe this. "I've got to see it," he muttered.

"Get a gun and hike over to the jail," Tully said. "You can see it when you get there."

He swung into the alley, circled the long building, and went on to Doc Wallace's office. Mulcahy was there, waiting for the medico to put on his coat and get his bag.

"We put Carradine to bed," the preacher said. "He seems as strong as when we left Broken Bell. It's a miracle."

"Don't leave Beth alone," Tully said. Wallace came out of the back room, and Tully asked: "How's Bob?"

"Fine. Seemed to settle down after you talked to him this morning." The medico tugged at his goatee, eyes on Tully. "I've got a notion to wake him up and tell him you've got Knapp in jail. Wasn't more'n a couple of hours ago that he said he'd give me odds you'd do it."

"Let him sleep," Tully said. "What's worrying me is how to keep Rocky there long enough to get enough evidence to hang him."

"How do you propose to do it?" Wallace asked.

"I dunno," Tully admitted. "Carradine promised to have a hearing in the morning if he's able. It'll be a devil of a note if he turns Rocky loose."

Wallace laughed softly. "I'll tell the judge he's got to stay in bed."

"You won't have to," Mulcahy said. "He's a sick man, too sick to hold court."

The old impatience crowded Tully. He was letting the star bind him, and he could not afford to let that happen, not when he was dealing with a man like Rocky Knapp. He said harshly: "What the hell does a court amount to at a time like this? Matt Quinn and his boys will bust Rocky out of jail if they can. I'll need help when they make their play."

"You'll get it," Wallace said, "but whether it'll be any good is another proposition."

"Drop in at the jail after you see Carradine," Tully said, and left the doctor's office.

He picked up the tray of food in the hotel dining room, ordered for himself, and took the tray to the jail. Furnes was there, sitting in Hoven's swivel chair, his feet on the desk. A grin creased his wrinkled face when he saw Tully.

"He's there, all right," Furnes said, "locked up real cozy, but he don't like it. He just told me."

"He'll like it less when he gets a rope on his neck," Tully said, and, unlocking the cell door, handed the tray to Knapp. "How soon do you expect your boys?"

"Any time. You know, Bain, Matt wanted to plug you before you ever got to the valley. I had some other notions, so I wouldn't let him, but it's a mistake I won't make again."

"You'll make a bigger mistake if you let 'em try to bust you out," Tully said. "If they do take you through that door, they'll be toting you feet first."

"I ain't much worried. Does Carradine figure he'll have a hearing in the morning?"

"You heard what he said."

"Then he'll turn me over to the grand jury, and then they'll try me. You and him will cook up some kind of frame and hang me. That it?"

"We don't need a frame."

"Think not? Hell, you haven't got anything to even hold me on. But if Carradine goes ahead, he'll hang himself. If I ever get into a witness chair, I'll blow the lid right off of this county."

"Maybe the judge is thinking the same thing." Tully stepped out of the cell and locked the door. "Fetch a gun, Jake?"

Furnes nodded and, lifting an ancient Navy Colt from his waistband, laid it on the desk. "Sure did."

"I'm gonna get a bait of grub." Tully motioned to the rack of guns on the wall. "Better check 'em over. See how much ammunition Bob has got around here. If you hear horses coming in, take a couple of shots at the moon and I'll come a-running."

Furnes gave him a worried look. "I don't cotton to being here alone when it starts."

"You won't," Tully said, and left the building.

XI

At this late hour the hotel dining room was empty. A place had been set near the kitchen door, and, as soon as Tully came in, a waitress brought his steak to him. She was a blonde girl who had grown up on the Svenson Ranch, a few miles upstream from town, one of the places Tully had passed on his way to Broken Bell. He remembered that when he had left, she was engaged to a neighbor boy.

"Married yet, Lissa?" he asked.

She gave him a wry grin. "Never heard of the word."

Glancing at her hand, he saw that she was not wearing a ring. He asked: "What happened?"

"Why should anyone get married in a country like this?" she demanded bitterly. "Any sense in raising babies so three or four of us can starve instead of two?"

"Rick still here?"

She shook her head. "He's in Harney County, riding for Pete French. I gave his ring back before he left. I wanted to get married but he said not until he had a stake, so he set out to get it at forty a month and beans."

"That why you gave his ring back?"

"It was then or never as far as I was concerned," she said. "I'll fetch your pie."

Turning, she left the dining room. Tully ate, his ears strained for Furnes's warning shot, but it had not come when he had finished his steak and the girl brought him a slab of dried apple pie and filled his coffee cup.

"Hard enough to make a living without having Carradine squeeze us to death," she said. "I hear you've got Rocky Knapp in jail. Won't do a bit of good. Carradine will turn him loose."

"Maybe not. What I need is some fighting men to keep Knapp in jail. What about your dad and your neighbors?"

"Save yourself a ride and don't ask them," she said tartly. "They wouldn't fight to keep their hats on their heads. Might be smarter to throw Carradine into jail to keep Knapp company."

"Maybe I will."

"No you won't. You wouldn't bust up your affair with Beth just to put Carradine where he belongs."

Tully rose and tossed a silver dollar on the table. "You've got it balled up a little. What charge would I arrest Carradine on?"

"I'll get your change."

"Keep it. I asked you a question."

She stared at him, unhappiness and frustration honing her temper thin. "You sound like Bob Hoven. Law, law, law. Well, I don't know anything about law, but I know what's right. Carradine was the finest man in the county for years. Loaned my dad and Rick's dad money when times were hard. Told Jake Furnes to carry them on his books. That's how he got things the way he wanted them. Now he'll own every ranch north of the creek by fall. He never backed Hoven up. If Hoven brought one of Knapp's men in for something, Carradine turned him loose. Claimed there wasn't enough evidence to hold him."

"You still haven't given me anything to arrest Carradine for."

"Isn't there such a thing as justice?" she cried.

"Law ain't always the same as justice," he said, and walked out, leaving her staring after him.

Tully stood on the boardwalk in front of the hotel and rolled a smoke, looking along the deserted street. He hated Carradine, hated him as he had never hated another man before in his life. Now a sense of futility gripped him, the same futility that must have plagued Bob Hoven for months.

It was like fighting a shadow. Carradine had frankly admitted he was at least indirectly responsible for the trouble, but no one else had heard him say it. Now Carradine was hiding behind his illness. There would be no hearing for Rocky Knapp in the morning. Probably not any morning.

Tully threw his cigarette into the street, finding no satisfaction in it. He went back to the jail and found Doc Wallace waiting for him.

"Carradine wants to see you," the medico said. "Mulcahy's staying with Beth."

"The devil with Carradine," Tully said savagely. "How bad off is he?"

"I don't know," Wallace admitted. "He's weak, but his heart's good. He might live for months."

"Ain't there anything wrong with him?"

"He's got a lump in his stomach and he hasn't been able to eat right for quite a while, but that don't mean he'll die tonight or next week." Wallace spread his hands. "Maybe he honestly thinks he's going to die in a few days. He's talked about it for a long time, and I never saw a man who was more afraid to die than he is."

"I suppose Mulcahy's talking to him about what it's like to go to purgatory," Tully snapped.

"Might be." Wallace picked up his black bag. "Better go see him."

"Why?"

"He's got something he wants to tell you." Wallace scratched his cheek. "Tully, I've learned a few things in the years I've practiced medicine. One of them is that a man's mind can make him as sick as his body. That's the way it is with Carradine, and I can't doctor him for that."

"You mean he's crazy?"

"In a way. I've got it figured out that he's wanted something all his life he's never had. Power, maybe. Respect. I don't know."

"He had respect," Tully said, "and he threw it out of the window."

"Did he really have it?" Wallace asked. "Or was it a simple matter of money that people wanted?"

Tully had never thought of it that way. He said: "All I know is that I respected him. That's what got under my hide the minute I hit town and heard he'd thrown in with the Knapps."

"But you're young and in love with Beth. You respected him because he was Beth's father and appeared to be honest." The medico shook his head. "I know these ranchers better than you ever will. I've brought their babies into the world and been with them when their loved ones died. They talk at times like that, honest talk. This was never a prosperous valley. Most of the men were like the Dorseys. No heroes. Just satisfied to get along. The more they got into debt to the judge, the more they distrusted him."

Wallace moved to the door and paused when Tully asked:

"How long would it take to get a new judge in here to hold court?"

"A long time. You'd have to prove Carradine was incompetent." Wallace jerked a hand toward the cell. "Too long to try that killing son-of-a-bitch."

"You ain't leavin' me here alone." Furnes jumped up from behind the desk. "Matt Quinn might show up while Tully is sashaying over to Carradine's place."

Tully wheeled to face him, remembering something. "Did you cut the Dorseys' credit off?"

The storekeeper lowered his gaze. "Yeah, I had to. I'd been carrying 'em for two years and I wasn't getting paid nothing. Carradine told me to cut 'em off. He said he wasn't loaning no more to 'em."

"You see how it is," Wallace said wearily. "Nobody, including the Dorseys, had any reason to respect Carradine. You can't like a man who grabs the food right off your plate from under your nose." He sighed. "Go on over and see Carradine. I'll stay till you get back."

"What good will it do?"

"None. But it'll make Beth feel better. That's worth walking over there for, isn't it?"

Tully hesitated, not wanting to go, then he remembered the waitress and what she had said about breaking up with the boy she was engaged to. The thought was never completely out of his mind that, if he lost Beth, there was nothing left for him. He remembered, too, what Beth had said on the way into town, that she couldn't forget what Carradine had done for her.

"All right," Tully said, and left the jail.

He walked rapidly to the Carradine house, his thoughts a bitter stream. He should have married Beth that morning; somehow he should have kept her from ever going back to Carradine. There had been no doubt of her love for Carradine when Tully had left three years ago, and that kind of love was hard to kill, even when Beth knew as much about Carradine as she did now.

He reached the Carradine house and yanked on the bell pull, thinking of the evening before when he had done the same thing and Carradine had come out and turned the world upside down for him. Then, quite suddenly, he realized how much his worry had gripped him.

Beth opened the door, and Tully went in without waiting for her to ask him. He closed the door and took her hands, looking down at her upturned face. He asked: "He hasn't fooled you, has he?"

"No, Tully," she said, surprised. "But things are different. He's anxious to talk to you."

Tully put his arms around her and pulled her to him. He kissed her, a long passionate kiss, trying to make it tell her he loved her. He let her go, still keeping her in his arms. He said: "We should have been married today."

She shook her head, smiling a little. "It's going to work out better this way. I told you I wanted a big wedding with all the fixings, a cake and pretty dress and everything. Now I'll have it." She gave him a push toward the stairs. "Go on up and see him."

"Nothing's changed, Beth."

"Yes, it has. Knapp's in jail, and he'll be convicted of murder. We don't have to hurry now. I mean, we can get married the way I've always wanted to."

He climbed the stairs, leaving her standing there, an undefined sense of uneasiness gripping him. After all that had happened, Carradine might still come out ahead. Beth, woman-like, wanted a big wedding, and Carradine was shrewd enough to work on her hunger for it. But worse than that, Beth did not seem to realize that Rocky Knapp was as much of a danger to them as he had ever been.

Tully saw that the door of Carradine's room was open, and Mulcahy was sitting by the bed, a Bible in his hand. The preacher rose when he saw Tully. He said: "Come in. I'll wait downstairs till you've had your talk."

Tully remained by the door until Mulcahy left the room. The preacher was gullible, Tully thought bitterly, plain fool gullible because he felt he must not judge another man. He had to forgive, had to think well of Carradine and let him go on raising hell the way he had been from the day he had thrown in with Rocky Knapp.

"Close the door," Carradine ordered.

Tully obeyed and came to the bed. "You've fooled Mulcahy, haven't you?"

"Why, yes," Carradine answered easily, "I believe I have. He's been praying for me, and he seems to think the Holy Spirit has taken possession."

"You sniveling, cheating son-of-a-bitch," Tully breathed. "Get out of that bed. I'm gonna throw you into the jug with Knapp."

"And lose Beth?" Carradine laughed softly. "She'd hate you if you did. You see, I admit I've been wrong, so I'm making restitution. Pull up a chair and I'll tell you about it."

Tully swore and sat down. "You mean you told Beth you'd been wrong, but you ain't sorry about a blamed thing, are you?"

Carradine reached to the stand beside the head of his bed and picked up a folded piece of paper. "I'm always sorry about failure. Your coming back has obliged me to make another run at this." He tapped the paper. "Inadvertently the preacher did me a favor when he brought up this business about where I got my money. He was wrong because it was honestly stolen by me, but I've told Beth it is hers."

"Why?"

"I told you I'd get her back, and I have. That was my way of doing it. Now you'll play with me because of her."

"What the devil makes you think I'll dance to your tune?"

"It's like I told you. All I need is the right price. I offered you two things, a cattle empire and Beth. The cattle empire may not appeal to you, but Beth does. A man as hungry for a woman as you are for Beth will get down on his knees to get her."

"She walked out of this house with me this morning," Tully said. "She'll do it again."

"No, and you won't tell her what I'm telling you because she'll doubt you. Doubt tempers a woman's love, Bain. You can't afford to take the chance."

"You're wrong. I'll. . . ."

"Just a minute." Carradine waved the paper at Tully. "Here is a deed to this house made out to Beth. I have also promised her that the money in the safe and the mortgages I hold will be handled the way she wants them. Restitution, I told you. It appeals to Beth. It took some talking and a few tears, but I have convinced her that the wrong things I did were motivated solely by my desire to protect her money."

"You chiseling, lying son-. . . ."

"Beth will not be persuaded by your name calling," Carradine interrupted. "I have assured her that I had planned to turn all my property over to her on her twenty-first birthday. A woman believes what she wants to believe regardless of logic. You will go back on Broken Bell. I'll see that you have the money you need to restock your range."

Carradine lay quite still, the side of his face against the pillow, dark eyes on Tully. Tully rose and walked to a window; he rolled and fired a cigarette. He could go down and tell Beth the truth, but there was a chance she'd think he was lying. Carradine had been right when he'd said Tully could not afford to make Beth doubt him. He wasn't sure she would. He wasn't sure she wouldn't, either. He swung back toward the bed, utterly miserable.

"What about Rocky?" Tully asked. "Quinn and his boys will try to bust him out of jail."

"I have confidence in you," Carradine said. "Perhaps a trial will not be necessary. As you can see, I'm too sick to hold court, and I shall be sick for some time, but the situation could be handled quite easily if Rocky was killed trying to break jail. In that case my health would improve."

"And I'll wind up sitting beside you," Tully said bitterly.

"That's about it. After your wedding which will be held in due time, we'll move Broken Bell cattle on to Box K range."

"You'll still be calling the turn."

Carradine was silent for a moment. Then he said: "Bain, I've lied and cheated and stolen, and I suppose that indirectly I've been responsible for murder, but there's one thing I've always been honest about. I love Beth. I won't lose her. Everything I do will be designed to make her trust me, so don't worry about me calling the turn."

"You're a good actor," Tully said bitterly.

Carradine smiled. "I pride myself on that talent, but what I've said about Beth is not acting."

"I don't savvy why you ever came out into the open."

"I'll admit I was afraid of Rocky," Carradine said, "and I got impatient, and tired of pretending, but I didn't realize it would hit Beth the way it has. I never dreamed she'd leave me as she did this morning."

"Doc says you might live quite a while. He says that what's wrong with you is in your head."

"Perhaps, but don't jump to the conclusion that I'm crazy. I told you I'm the sanest man in the valley. Remember that."

Tully ground out his cigarette. He was trapped, and at this moment he could think of nothing to do but play it out. The immediate problem was Rocky Knapp.

"How did you honestly steal that money?" Tully asked.

"You might call it a confidence game. I invested in a few rough diamonds and salted a piece of ground. I sold stock in my company, but it blew up and I found it expedient to leave the country. But the knowledge will do you no good, and Beth won't believe you. I've told her the money was her mother's. Remember that."

Tully walked to the door. He said: "I'll tell Beth to go ahead with her wedding plans."

"By all means," Carradine said pleasantly.

Tully went down the stairs. Beth and Mulcahy were waiting for him in the living room. He paused in the doorway, looking at them, uncertain how much to tell them and haunted by his fear of losing Beth again. She rose and came to him.

"You see, Tully?" she asked. "He isn't fighting our marriage now."

"This morning you said we'd make our lives without him."

"I thought we had to." She frowned. "Whatever he's done that was wrong, I can't forget, but he has taken care of me and he has never been cross with me except about you. Now he's sick and he needs me, so I can't just walk out on him. Can't you understand that?"

"You're tired," he said. "You better go to bed."

She nodded. "I think I will." Still she lingered, her eyes on him. "I'm glad I went out to Broken Bell, and you know there was only one reason I went. I . . . I don't want to quarrel with you about anything."

"We're not quarreling," he said.

She gave him a quick kiss and walked past him and went up the stairs, calling back: "Good night."

"Good night," Tully said, watching her until she disappeared.

Mulcahy rose and walked to where Tully stood. "It's a knotty business."

"Not so knotty. Carradine is a crook and you're helping him hurt Beth."

"Perhaps I am," Mulcahy said, his red face troubled. "I don't know, but I do know that there are times when the Lord works in a mysterious way."

"It's a mighty funny religion that makes an honest man blind," Tully said hotly. "This afternoon at Broken Bell you were sure. . . ."

"I know, I know." Mulcahy spread his big hands. "But I might have been wrong. When we got here, I prayed over him and read the Bible, and he changed. I saw it, Tully. Strength seemed to flow back into his body. He said that for the first time in his life he felt at peace. I'd like to believe he was converted. It is not for me to say he wasn't."

"You're a fool," Tully muttered, "and you're the last man in the valley I ever thought I'd say that to."

"Marry Beth." Mulcahy laid a hand on Tully's shoulder. "We'll work this out. Let's see what the future holds."

"The future won't change him being a crook!" Tully shouted. "If I told you what he told me, you wouldn't believe me, would you?"

"I'm not sure I would," the preacher admitted. "You're filled with too much bitterness to see anything clearly."

Mulcahy didn't say it, Tully thought, but he might as well have put it into words. Tully's past was against him. The preacher was thinking he was the same wild kid he'd been when he'd left the valley, his turbulent emotions still ruling him.

"Oh, the devil," Tully said, and turned on his heel. He paused with a hand on the doorknob and looked back. "Don't leave Beth alone tonight."

"I'll stay here," Mulcahy said.

Tully went out into the darkness, knowing it was just as well he had not told Beth what Carradine had said. Well, he'd play it out. As Mulcahy had said, they'd have to see what the future held, and the future was not on Carradine's side. Sooner or later the truth would overcome Beth's binding sense of obligation.

Wallace rose when Tully came into the sheriff's office. He picked up his black bag, asking: "Learn anything?"

"Nothing except that Mulcahy's a bigger fool than I thought he was."

"A good kind of fool," Wallace said. "You could learn a little from him."

The doctor walked out, leaving Tully smarting under the mild reprimand. He went outside, ignoring Furnes's questioning stare. He rolled and smoked a cigarette, unconsciously listening for the drumbeat of incoming horses, but there was no sound except the clack of the doctor's shoes on the walk, then that died. The street was bright in the moonlight except where shadows of the false fronts darkened the dust, and now and then a chill blast of wind rushed down the valley, crying around the corners and eaves of the buildings.

Tully flipped his cigarette stub into the street, morosely watching the glow until it winked out. He had never felt as completely alone as he did now, and he thought of Dave Lowrie who had succeeded in living apart from the rest of the valley with only his riders for company. Bob Hoven, too, must have been cursed by that same loneliness, beaten down by his inability to punish those who deserved punishment.

For a moment Tully was tempted to tear the star off his shirt and throw it into the street, to get his black out of the stable, and ride a hundred miles before he stopped. But he couldn't and the moment passed. He was no longer a free man because he had something to fight for that was worth the fighting. So he'd keep Rocky Knapp in jail till he rotted; he'd give Carradine all the rope he needed in the hope he'd finally hang himself.

Tully turned into the office. Furnes still sat behind the desk, patiently pulling on a black briar. Tully said: "You knew the Dorseys would starve when you cut off their credit."

Suddenly angry, Furnes jerked the pipe out of his mouth. "Don't start hoorawing me again, mister."

"You could hold all the guts in the valley in a spoon," Tully said with biting contempt.

"Go get somebody else to sit here for bullet bait." Furnes rose. "Just where would you start looking?"

Tully was ashamed then, for the very fact that Furnes was here set him above most of the other townsmen and small ranchers who would have refused any part in this. He said: "I'm sorry, Jake. I'm going out to the Anchor 9 in the morning. I don't reckon Quinn will show up in daylight."

"I ain't real proud of myself," Furnes said, "if that's what you want to hear. I've been under Carradine's thumb the same as everybody else. I ain't so sure you're not, either."

Tully was too tired to argue the point. He said: "I'm going to bed. Didn't get much sleep last night. After three, four hours you wake me up and you can sleep."

Furnes nodded and Tully went into the small room beside the office where Bob Hoven slept when he had a prisoner in jail. Tully lay down and was asleep at once.

It seemed only a moment later that Furnes shook him awake, whispering: "A rider's coming in."

Tully roused at once, aware of thin morning light that was washing in through the single window. "You let me sleep all night."

"I figured you needed it. I told you a rider was coming into town."

"Just one?"

"I think so. Riding slow."

Tully rose and drew his gun. "Get a scatter-gun off the wall.

Wayne D. Overholser

Might be a trick. Quinn wouldn't send one man in to do the job."

He crossed the office to the door and slid out, moving fast, and stood with his back to the wall. The rider was visible now in the gray light, slumped over the saddle horn as if he were hurt. Still Tully stood motionlessly, waiting. He could not yet recognize the man, and he had a feeling that this was bait to draw him into the open. The shadows along the street might be covering the rest of the Box K crew.

Then the rider was opposite Tully and an involuntary cry broke out of him. It was Ed Dorsey. Tully holstered his gun and ran into the street, calling—"Ed!"—and was aware that Jake Furnes stood beside him.

Ed reined up and sat his saddle as if he had lost the power of movement. Tully, staring at him, had the impression the man was sleeping with his eyes open. Tully said: "Get down, Ed."

"Yeah, sure," Ed muttered, and swung out of the saddle.

He lurched sideways and would have fallen if Tully had not gripped his arm and steadied him. If it had been any other man, Tully would have sworn he was drunk. He said—"Tie his horse, Jake."—and led Ed into the office. He jerked the swivel chair from the desk and eased Ed into it.

"Lon's dead." Ed wiped a hand across his face. "Shot in the back before we got to Stone Saddle. We didn't ride fast enough."

He was dazed. Tully remembered what Knapp had said. At the time Tully hadn't been sure the man was telling the truth. Now there could be no doubt of it. Regardless of what Lon had done, his death was murder.

"You see who did it?" Tully asked.

"No. They fired from the top of a ridge. Lon was dead before he fell out of the saddle." Ed rubbed his face again. "I buried him the best I could. I came back. Thought I could do something. Help you some way."

154

"Sure, you can help me," Tully said. "You get some sleep now. We'll figure out what to do after you wake up."

He got Ed out of the chair and led him into the side room. Ed fell across the cot, completely exhausted, and was asleep at once. When Tully went back into the office, Furnes had come in from the street.

Tully glanced at his watch. The sun would be up soon. He said: "Let Ed sleep. I'm going out to see Dave Lowrie. I don't reckon we'll hear anything of Rocky's boys till dark."

Furnes made no protest when Tully left the office and turned along the street toward the stable.

XII

Tully was aware as he left town that his chance of getting help from Dave Lowrie was a slim one, that his riding to the Anchor 9 was a last-ditch gesture he had to make because there was no other place he could turn to for adequate help. He tried to put Beth and Carradine out of his mind as he rode, tried to focus his thinking on Matt Quinn and guess what the man's play would be.

The fact that the Box K hands had not tried to break Knapp out of jail during the night did not prove anything. With Pete dead and Rocky in jail, Quinn would be the natural leader of the pack. Because his loyalty was beyond question, Tully knew he would come sooner or later.

There must have been some reason for his not coming during the night. Turning it over in his mind, Tully could think of only one thing. Quinn knew Tully would be tired and he'd probably stay awake all night expecting a visit from the Box K crew, but Tully wouldn't be able to stay awake two nights in a row. So they'd probably come tonight, counting on his being so drugged by sleep that a surprise attack would be effective. Quinn, having nothing but contempt for the townsmen, would discount any help Tully could get from the men like Jake Furnes.

Then, in spite of himself, Tully's thoughts turned to Beth and Judge Carradine. He did not know how long it would take Beth to get her dress made, to have a cake baked, and arrange for all the details that a fancy wedding took. But the time that those things took could be endured if it made Beth any happier. The big question that nagged Tully's mind concerned Carradine, not Beth.

Tully had no idea what turn Carradine's sly thinking would take, but he could not overcome the fear that somehow the man would find a way to prevent his marrying Beth. As the miles fell behind, a sense of futility grew in Tully. Carradine's trickery was something he did not know how to fight.

The sun had been up an hour or more when Tully forded the creek just above the Anchor 9 headquarters. Now that he was here, he began to question his judgment in coming and leaving Jake Furnes to guard Knapp. Ed Dorsey in his dazed condition would be no help. Bob Hoven was in bed. Mulcahy had been up all night and he'd be asleep. The chances were good that Doc Wallace would be called out of town as he often was.

Well, there was nothing for Tully to do but get this over with and light out for town. Win or lose, Tully wouldn't be here till dark, and he assured himself that Quinn would not show up until evening or later. Still, no one could be certain what Quinn would do, and a sense of uneasiness began to plague Tully.

When Tully rode into the Anchor 9 yard, he saw that the crew was saddling up and Lowrie was not in sight. Slim Taylor let out a whoop when he recognized Tully, yelling: "Boys, take a look at that star! I'll bet it's made out of pure tin."

They waited for him to ride up, grinning uncertainly. Tully said: "I need four good men about the size of you boys."

"Want some help branding calves, I'll bet," Slim said. "Or maybe you've got some tough bronc's to break. Curly here is the best bronc'. . . ."

"You know damned well what I want," Tully interrupted. "I've got Rocky Knapp in the jug and I'm expecting his boys to make a visit. I want some help to keep him."

Their grins died. Slim turned his horse and mounted. He said: "Sorry. We're plumb busy. Just got our orders."

"Whatever you think of the Box K bunch," Tully said, "you've got to admit they're damned good men. I was hoping I'd find some more out here who'd match 'em."

The Anchor 9 hands stared at him truculently for a moment, then the others mounted. Slim said: "We ain't pulling nobody's irons out of the fire. When the sign's right, we'll match anybody at any time."

They would have ridden off if Tully hadn't asked: "Where's Lowrie?"

Slim motioned toward the cook shack. "In there, having his tenth cup of coffee."

"Wait till I see him," Tully urged. "Maybe I am wasting my time, but give me a chance. It's for him as well as the rest of us."

Slim laughed. "Well now, that's quite a notion you've got. All right, we'll wait."

Tully rode across the yard to the cook shack, a low log structure just west of the house. The door opened before he could step down and Dave Lowrie stood there, a small, wiry man who looked no older than when he had come to the valley five years before. He said courteously: "Come in and have breakfast, Bain." He jerked a hand toward his crew. "Get on your way."

"Hold on," Tully said. "I'm out here to get help." He indicated his star. "I'm serving as deputy for Bob Hoven."

"Help you say." A small smile touched the corners of Lowrie's mouth. "Been a long time since I've heard that word. Well, if the county needs some deputies, it can pay them. My boys work for Anchor 9."

"Before you let 'em go," Tully urged, "let me tell you what's happened."

"Sure, tell me," Lowrie said. "Maybe I'll give you a hand, but I won't send my boys into a shooting ruckus that ain't no concern of ours." He motioned again, and this time his voice was sharp when he said: "If you don't get out of here, you'll meet yourself riding in for supper."

Tully stepped down, knowing that this was just about what he had expected. Still, he was disappointed. He said: "It's time we were working together instead of letting Rocky Knapp knock over a ranch at a time."

"The thought has occurred to me," Lowrie said. "Slim said you were riding out here to see me. I'm a mite curious about what you figure can be done."

Tully, glancing over his shoulder, saw that Slim and the others were riding south across the sage flat. He went into the cook shack and sat down on a bench at the table, doubting his wisdom in staying. He would have started back for Starbuck if Lowrie hadn't said he might give a hand. That was one thing he had not expected.

Lowrie nodded at the Chinese cook who was hovering over the big range at the end of the room. "Fry some more flapjacks, Chang. Fetch the coffee pot over here." He sat down across the table from Tully. "Funny thing. I've been here five years and folks have let me alone, so I've let them alone. Now they want help."

"Me," Tully said. "Not them."

"Yeah, that is a little different," Lowrie admitted. "Slim told me you done a good job on Pete Knapp. Well, let's have the yarn."

Tully gave Lowrie a straight look, curious about the man's

interest. He had seen Lowrie a few times before he'd left the valley; he had spoken to him, but he had never really talked with him. Now it occurred to him that what Lowrie had said about folks leaving him alone might account for the way he had lived apart from the rest of the valley people.

Something about Lowrie's lean, bronzed face held Tully's attention. In spite of his small size, there was an air of strength about him, in the slant of his long jaw and his steady blue eyes. He was more friendly than hostile, Tully thought. He was simply waiting to be convinced.

The cook filled Lowrie's coffee cup and, reaching across the table, poured coffee into the cup in front of Tully. He padded back to the stove to stand over the big frying pan with its load of flapjacks. Tully took a drink of the steaming, black coffee and set the cup back on the table.

"I need a posse and you sent your men off," Tully said. "Not much use in talking."

"I'm worth the four of them," Lowrie said without the slightest hint of brag in his voice. "I seldom go to town, but my boys do and they fetch back the gossip. I've heard about your dad and I know why you left the country. If anybody else had come out here squalling for help, I'd kick him off the place." He tapped the table top. "Some men fight and some just quit. And some talk a good fight, but it turns out to be hot air. I'm wondering about you."

Angry, Tully slammed a fist against the table, jarring the dishes. "I've got Rocky Knapp in jail. You think hot air done that?"

Surprised, Lowrie said: "The hell." Then he grinned. "Tell me about it."

The cook brought a plate of flapjacks to the table. Tully reached for the syrup and covered them, wondering how much to tell. He ate, talking slowly and telling as little about Beth as he could. Lowrie leaned forward, listening closely. When Tully finished, Lowrie motioned for the coffee again.

"I don't like it," Lowrie said. "I don't like anybody getting too big for his britches. A man like Rocky Knapp never gets enough to satisfy him."

Tully rose. "I've got a stake here. I hate like the devil to lose it."

"Money and a crooked court." Lowrie stared at the coffee cup the cook had filled again. "And a wolf pack like Knapp's. Makes a hard combination to beat." He looked up. "I'm wondering about Carradine. I'd guess he was telling the truth when he said he figured on using the girl to kick you into line."

"Right now my job is keeping Knapp in jail," Tully said, "or if I had a posse I could count on, I'd go after Quinn and Lytell. I reckon Lon's murder would be enough. Either way, Carradine doesn't count for a few days. Maybe it'll blow up before he does."

"If he'd do his part in getting a rope on Knapp's neck," Lowrie said, "he'd count plenty."

"I don't think he will," Tully said, "but I still aim to keep Rocky in jail. If he got out, I couldn't fetch him back myself."

Tully turned toward the door. Lowrie said: "You ain't in no big hurry." When Tully swung back to face him, Lowrie went on. "I was never one to risk my hide for men who didn't have the guts it takes to fight for themselves, but I might take a chance on you being different. I've got one question. From my standpoint, is there any reason I should back you?"

"A good one," Tully said, "besides cleaning this valley up which is to your interest as well as mine. If I can hold Broken Bell and get some land on Knapp's side of the creek, we could build a dam so you and everybody else would have the water you need when you need it. It's the only way to develop the valley."

160

Lowrie gave him a flat-lipped grin. "I've heard that dam talk ever since I've been here, and it makes sense except for one thing. Who's got any money to build it except Carradine?"

"We wouldn't need much money once we get this other business settled," Tully said. "Just some tools and dynamite that we could wangle out of Furnes. The little fellers will work if they ain't scared somebody is gonna dry-gulch 'em."

Lowrie rose, nodding. "I'd thought of that, too, but it takes somebody to kick them in the tail. You might be the one, except that you're broke and your range is cleaned off and Carradine will close you out in the fall. Then where will we stand?"

"Maybe he won't live that long. Anyhow, we've got to do one thing at a time. We can't do anything as long as Rocky's swinging a wide loop and dry-gulching men who are in his way."

Lowrie scratched his chin, still undecided. "Bob Hoven could have stopped this if he hadn't been touched on what's legal and what ain't." He gave Tully his flat-lipped grin again. "I reckon you ain't bogged down in the fine points of the law."

"I wouldn't have Rocky in jail if I was."

"I reckon not. Now suppose Mulcahy is right about the money belonging to your girl and suppose Carradine is lying about his confidence game. And suppose Mulcahy can prove his hunch. Would Beth take a chance on backing the dam if it works out so she can?"

"You bet she would," Tully said quickly. "Broken Bell will be part hers when we're married."

"I'll go along," Lowrie said. "A man has to make a stand sometime. Looks like this is it. I'll get my guns and saddle up."

Dazed, Tully watched Lowrie walk around the table and leave the cook shack. He had not been sure at any time that he was convincing Lowrie.

The cook asked blandly: "Suplised?"

"Yeah," Tully breathed. "I sure am."

"Boss a good man," the cook said. "Leal good."

Tully went outside and waited beside his horse. There was no wind now and the morning promised a warm day. From somewhere out in the sage a meadowlark gave its sweet song. The smell of spring was in the air at last, Tully thought, and the grass would start. Then he saw Lowrie come across the yard from the house. He wore two black-butted .45s, the cartridge belts crossed, and both guns were tied low on the man's thighs the way a gunslinger carries them.

Lowrie nodded as if he understood Tully's thoughts. "You'd be surprised if you knew the name I used to go by, but it ain't important." He frowned as if his mind had reluctantly turned back to a smoky past. "When I came here, I thought I'd never wear my guns again, but I wasn't counting on Rocky Knapp. Maybe a man never gets to the place where he stops fighting. I've just been fooling myself."

He went on to the corral. Tully, staring at Lowrie's straight back, felt a quick glow of pride. He was responsible for Dave Lowrie's buckling his guns on again. Now he believed what Lowrie had said, that he was worth the four men who rode for him.

A moment later they took the road to town, keeping their horses at a ground-eating pace. Neither felt inclined to talk. Then, with the sun well up in the sky and the buildings of Starbuck directly ahead of them, a gunshot in town made a sudden, thunder-like sound. Tully's instant thought was that they were too late, for they were still some distance from Starbuck.

Tully glanced at Lowrie and Lowrie nodded. "Took too long to convince me, sounds like."

They cracked steel to their horses and went on in a run, clumps of sagebrush flashing by in a gray blur. When they reached Main Street, they saw the knot of townsmen in front of the jail, and Furnes wheeled toward them, swinging an arm in an imperative gesture.

When they reined up, Furnes yelled: "Quinn and his boys rode into town quiet-like and took Knapp out without cracking a cap! I didn't know a thing about it till they'd done the job."

But there had been a gunshot. For a moment it made no sense to Tully. He stared down at their upturned faces, a sudden wild rage burning through him. They'd let Knapp go without any kind of a fight.

Bob Hoven was there, pale-faced and trembling, his hair disheveled. He put a hand to his forehead. "I was in bed. I didn't know what was. . . ."

"My fault," Furnes broke in. "I didn't think anything would happen in broad daylight. You didn't, either, Tully."

"Where were you?" Tully demanded.

"In the store. I left Ed. . . ."

"Where is he?"

"Inside. They knocked him cold with a gun barrel before he could do anything, I reckon. I had to get my store open. . . ."

"I heard a shot. Where was it?"

"At Carradine's house," Furnes said. "We ain't gone over there."

"Rabbits," Lowrie said in a contemptuous, bitter voice. "Where'd Knapp's bunch go?"

"They left town a little while ago," Furnes said, "but we figured some of 'em might still be at Carradine's. We didn't want to run into no trouble. . . ."

Tully wheeled his horse, knowing that if he stayed here, he'd do something he'd regret. Then he thought of Beth and fear squeezed breath out of him. He hit his gelding with his spurs; he rocketed down the street and around the corner, catching sight of Mulcahy coming down the street in a lumbering run.

Lowrie brought his horse up beside Tully's and they reined to a stop together in front of the Carradine house. Tully hit the ground and sprinted up the walk, Lowrie falling a step behind. Tully crossed the porch in long strides, yanked the door open, and went in.

"Beth?" Tully shouted. "Beth, are you here?"

Lowrie was beside him then, both of them standing motionlessly in the gloomy hall. Again Tully called: "Beth?" There was no answer, except the echoes of his shout that were thrown back at him from the deserted house.

XIII

If Tully Bain lived to be a thousand years old, he would never survive a longer moment than this. His heart was hammering in great, sledge-like blows; his lungs were empty and for a moment he was unable to suck air back into them.

The door into the living room was open. No one was there. When the last echo of his frantic shout died, he could hear nothing except the rattling of an upstairs window in a sudden gust of wind. He felt Lowrie's hand on his shoulder, heard the Anchor 9 man say: "They wouldn't kidnap a woman. She's around here somewhere, maybe too scared to answer."

"Go upstairs," Tully said hoarsely.

He went along the hall, opening doors and slamming them shut, mentally cursing Furnes and Bob Hoven and Ed Dorsey and all of them for letting this happen. He heard Lowrie go up the stairs two at a time, heard the crack of boots overhead. Then Tully reached Carradine's study. Beth lay motionlessly on the floor, her hands flung out at her sides, a faint trickle of blood making a dark streak on her forehead.

Tully thought: *They've killed her.* He gripped the doorjamb, the room tipping and whirling before him. Odd bits of disjointed thought crowded his mind. She would never kiss him again, never tell him she loved him. He could have married her the morning before. He should have stayed in town. Matt Quinn had outsmarted him after all.

Then the thought came to Tully that he had no reason to live. It was a flat, empty world, without vitality, without meaning. Lowrie came down the stairs and along the hall, and still Tully stood there, unable to move, right hand gripping the doorjamb, knuckles white. Lowrie was directly behind him then, looking past him, and he swore in a low bitter tone.

"She's dead," Tully muttered. "She's dead."

Lowrie shoved past him and, kneeling beside Beth, picked up a hand and felt of her wrist. He dropped her hand, very carefully lifted her from the floor, and carried her to the couch. He walked back to Tully.

"Come out of it, Bain," Lowrie said. "She's all right. Just knocked out."

But his words made no impression on Tully's dazed mind. He started to turn, mumbling: "She's dead." Lowrie grabbed an arm and jerked him around; he slapped Tully sharply on one cheek, and then the other, rocking his head.

"Come out of it, Bain!" Lowrie shouted. "I tell you she's all right!"

Instinctively Tully drew back his fist to hit Lowrie, then the other man's words made sense and what had seemed like a heavy weight pressing against his forehead was lifted. He lunged past Lowrie to the couch; he fell on his knees beside it, and, grabbing Beth's limp hand, placed a fingertip on her wrist. The pulse beat was steady and regular.

He leaned back and looked at Lowrie, both hands gripping the edge of the couch. He said: "She is alive."

Lowrie wasn't paying any attention to him. He stood in the middle of the room, looking around, and now he pointed to a pool of blood on the floor. He said: "Somebody got hurt. Carradine ain't in the house. Reckon it was him?"

Tully didn't say anything. He remained there on his knees

beside the couch, staring at Beth's pale face. He felt of her head. There was a big lump just above her forehead. The skin had been broken and the trickle of blood had come from that. She must have been slugged by a gun barrel.

"Look," Lowrie said. "They've been through Carradine's safe. What would they take?"

Tully turned his head. The safe was open, a pile of papers and envelopes on the floor below it. He said: "Carradine kept his mortgages and his money there. He didn't say how much, but I think it was quite a bit."

Beth stirred. Tully swung back; he saw her eyes open and stare blankly at him, and for a moment he thought she didn't know him. Then she smiled and whispered: "Tully."

For the first time as long as he could remember he wanted to cry. He bowed his head, blinking. The moment of shock had passed and he began to tremble, his body weak. He had been so sure he had lost her. He took her hands, waiting a moment until he could control his emotions, then he asked: "Are you all right, Beth?"

"My head aches." She drew a hand away and gingerly felt of the lump on her head. "Knapp hit me. Dad tried to fight and Quinn shot him. I guess I jumped onto Knapp and then the sky fell on me." She looked past Tully. "Hello, Nat."

Tully had not been aware of Mulcahy's presence until then. He stared at the preacher's troubled face, then saw the others who had stopped in the hall, Furnes and Bob Hoven and a few more.

"I should have stayed here," Mulcahy said with keen regret, "but I'd been up all night and I went home to sleep. I didn't suppose there would be any trouble during the day."

"Neither did I," Furnes said quickly as if wanting to defend himself before he was accused of negligence. "I can't figure it out."

"I'll get my wife to stay with Beth," Mulcahy said.

Hoven came into the room. He said wearily: "I'll go after them. They must have taken Carradine."

Tully rose, motioning to the stableman. "Jeff, take our horses to the livery barn and saddle up the best animals you've got."

Jeff wheeled and ran out of the house. Lowrie had come to stand beside Mulcahy. "Bain and me will go. You stay here, Hoven. You're in no shape to ride."

"It'll take more'n two of you . . . ," Hoven began.

"No," Tully said. "Two of us will be enough. Go back to bed, Bob. Where's Doc?"

"Missus Malone is having her baby," Furnes said. "They came after Doc early this morning."

"Beth needs him . . . ," Tully began.

"I'm all right," she said.

"I'll get my wife, Tully," Mulcahy said, and this time left the room.

"We'd better go," Lowrie said.

Still Tully stood there, looking at Beth. She smiled and held her arms out to him. "Whatever you do, Tully, come back."

He stooped and kissed her, her arms circling his neck in a frantic embrace, then she let him go, whispering: "I love you, Tully. No matter what happens, remember that."

"It's the one good thing I've got to remember," he said, and, turning, pushed his way through the crowd in the hall and left the house.

Now a cold fury gripped Tully. He had never felt this way before in his life; he had never wanted to kill a man the way he wanted to kill Rocky Knapp. He strode across the vacant lot toward the stable, Lowrie keeping step with him and looking sideways at him.

"When a man's as mad as you are, he ain't very smart," Lowrie said. "Get hold of yourself."

"I'm bringing Knapp in," Tully choked. "I'm bringing him in tied across his saddle."

"You've got a star. . . ."

"The devil with it. You heard what she said. He slugged her."

They went into the stable from the alley. Jeff had saddled two geldings, a buckskin and a sorrel. He said: "They'll get you there. Coming back is your job."

"Tully."

Ed Dorsey stood in the doorway, a red bandanna tied around his head.

Tully had a foot in the stirrup ready to mount. He paused, asking: "What?"

"I'm going, too," Ed said. "I've got more reason to go than anyone."

"Hell," Lowrie said in a cranky voice, "we won't have any time to look out for cripples."

"He can go." Tully swung into the saddle, thinking about Lon. "It's like he says. He's got more to square up than anyone else."

Lowrie shrugged and mounted. Ed came along the runway to the stall that held his horse, his face gray and pinched with the habitual good humor gone from it. He would never be the same man again, Tully thought. Then he wondered if anything would be the same—ever? As Mulcahy had said, it was a long trail back.

Tully and Lowrie left the silent town behind them, Ed Dorsey catching up a moment later. Presently Lowrie said: "Nobody seemed surprised that I was with you."

"They will be tomorrow," Tully said. "After they think about it."

Lowrie laughed softly. "I reckon. Well, it's been a long time since I set out on a manhunt. Seems like you live a piece of life, and then a long time later, you live it over again." He glanced at

Tully's bleak face. "It's an old pattern, but I have to keep reminding myself of it. Some men can fight and some can't, and that's the way of it. Bob Hoven will never be much good again. You know that?"

"Hadn't thought of it."

"You will after this is over. He's an old man now and he'll give up his star. Maybe get a job with Jake Furnes."

"You're wrong," Tully said. "He had a lot of guts. Took plenty to side me the other night when I was tangling with Pete."

Lowrie shrugged. "Maybe, but I'm thinking that, when you left the valley, you had him sized up the way a kid does somebody he likes. I don't think he ever was the right man for the job."

They were silent then, Tully knowing that Lowrie might be right. But that wasn't important now. Hoven had done all he could. Tully was certain of that, and it seemed to him that Hoven had a right to give up his star if he wanted to.

Tully glanced back at Ed who was riding behind them, hunched forward in the saddle, one hand gripping the horn, his head bowed. Tully thought about how it had been up there in the mountains, Lon shot out of his saddle without warning and Ed digging a shallow grave and kneeling there while he prayed over him. The long trail back. No, it would never be the same for any of them.

They were opposite the Svenson place, the home of the blonde girl who worked in the hotel dining room. Upstream a quarter of a mile was the O'Brien Ranch where Rick, the boy she had been engaged to, had grown up. They were alike, the Svensons and the O'Briens and the others, hanging on till fall when Carradine would close them out and hoping for a miracle that would save them. And Tully found some satisfaction in the thought that he and Lowrie and Ed Dorsey were riding to bring that miracle about.

"I don't savvy why you came with me," Tully said. "Not the real reason."

Lowrie gave him a tight-lipped grin. "I'll tell you, although it won't make sense to anybody else. I've been a stranger in this valley for five years. I figured this would change things. If it don't, I'll get out."

Tully nodded, remembering that Doc Wallace had been certain Lowrie would not help. Being the kind of man he was, Dave Lowrie was incapable of making his first gesture. The valley people, always slow to accept a newcomer, had let him alone and he had let his neighbors alone.

Lowrie swore in an excited voice. "There's a body yonder. Looks like Carradine."

Tully saw the man, a few feet from the road and almost hidden by the tall sagebrush. He reined off the road, Lowrie following him. The instant Tully stepped down, he saw that Carradine was still alive. The lawyer lay on his back, a dark splotch of blood covering most of the front of his white shirt.

Tully knelt beside him, asking: "Judge, can you hear me?"

Carradine turned his head, dark eyes on Tully a moment before he said: "Bain! You're a devil, haunting me while I'm dying. It'll be easy for you now with me gone."

"Why did they shoot you?"

"Rocky got boogery, sitting in jail. Just wanted to get out of the country, but he was bound to take my money with him. Made me open my safe. I had a gun inside, but I didn't get a chance to use it."

"Why did they take you with them?"

"Thought they could use me to bargain with you if their luck went sour, but I fell out of the saddle and they went on. Hell, they didn't know, did they? I'm the last man you'd bargain for."

"They've got the money?"

"It's in Rocky's saddlebags." Carradine's eyes were glazed

with death, and he must have known he had only a moment of life left. He raised a hand and gripped Tully's arm. "I've hated you a long time because Beth loved you. I couldn't stand sharing her love with anybody."

"You tried to make a deal with me."

"I aimed to use you for a while, but sooner or later I'd have killed you."

"You were going to make her marry Pete."

"But I wouldn't have let her go through with it. I'd have stopped it, some way." His claw-like fingers dug into Tully's arm. "Tell Beth I loved her. She was all I had left of my wife. I wanted her to have everything. I wanted to be the biggest man in the world for her. Promise you'll tell her."

"I'll tell her."

Carradine's hand slid off Tully's arm. "Rocky's going to burn your place. They aren't far ahead. They're leaving the country." His eyes were closed. "I'll see you in hell. I'll be stoking up the furnace . . . when . . . you come . . . through . . . the door."

Then Carradine was dead. Tully rose, staring down at the man's yellow, lifeless face, and for the first time he understood him. Carradine's possessive love had been a perverse force, making him do things Beth had hated and still blinding him to her feelings.

"Don't tell anybody about this," Tully said hoarsely. "Let Beth think as well of him as she can."

"Sure. . . ." Lowrie hesitated, and then added: "Love. Funny word. Does funny things."

Tully turned to his horse and mounted. Ed Dorsey had remained in the road, indifferent to what Carradine had to say. He had been too far away to hear. Tully said: "We'll ask Svenson to take the body in."

"Let the coyotes have him," Lowrie said.

171

Tully shook his head. "He doesn't deserve no better, but Beth does."

XIV

They were traveling fast when they passed the road that branched south toward the Box K. They were not far from Broken Bell now, and there was a question in Tully's mind about how to play it. Probably Carradine had told the truth when he'd said Knapp planned to burn Broken Bell, but the time element was an uncertainty. Knapp would pick up a few things at the Box K before he left the country, horses at least and enough grub to last a few days.

Tully guessed that Knapp and his men would strike westward across the mountains and try to lose themselves in the high desert. It was an empty land with no one to tell of their passage, and Knapp knew the location of the few water holes that were there. Later they would strike south toward Lakeview, and cross the state line into California, or angle eastward into Nevada.

Considering it carefully, Tully realized that it was impossible to follow Knapp's devious thinking. They might keep riding westward and cross the Cascades, following the Santiam Pass into the Willamette Valley. Or they might swing north to the Columbia and cross over into Washington. In any case, once they were out of Bowstring Valley, the chase would be long and difficult. Tully couldn't let them go. They had Beth's money, and Ed Dorsey would follow them until they killed him. But there was another reason that had become increasingly important. Tully Bain was the law.

Troubled, Tully glanced at Lowrie. "What do you think?"

"We'll try Broken Bell first," Lowrie said as if he had thought this through.

They went on, following the wheel tracks that led to Broken Bell, the pines crowding the road. The day before Tully had made a cautious swing to the top of the ridge. There was no time for caution now, although Tully was fully aware that they might be riding into a bushwhack trap. Lowrie seemed oblivious to any danger. It was, Tully thought, an old game with him.

Lowrie must have sensed Tully's thoughts, for he said: "They won't figure on us being this close. The question is whether we're close enough to surprise 'em. We'd better get a move on."

Tully motioned to Ed Dorsey who was still riding behind them, and they brought their horses up into a run, hoofs beating into the soft, rain-soaked earth. It was cool and damp here in the pines, limbs forming a cover overhead that strained the sunlight so that a sharp ray broke through only here and there to brighten the darkness of shadow.

Tully caught the smell of smoke before they reached the clearing that held Broken Bell's buildings, and he cursed Rocky Knapp for his vengeful spirit that had made him take time from his flight to do this. Then they were out of the pines. Horses were grouped in the yard, three men holding them. The house was in flames, and in one sweeping glance Tully saw Knapp and Quinn come out of the barn, smoke trailing them. An instant later Lytell appeared behind them.

One of the men holding the horses let out a squall. Lowrie, riding low in the saddle, threw the first shot, knocking one man flat on his back among the plunging horses. Tully got Lytell before he had a chance to fire, and Ed Dorsey, yelling like a crazy man, came up on Tully's left, his first shot taking Matt Quinn in the chest.

The other two men who had been holding the horses broke for the cover of a shed. The horses, boogered by the firing, had scattered. The surprise was complete. Lowrie had been right in assuming the Box K men had not expected anyone to be this close behind them.

In that first burst of firing, Tully and his friends had made the odds equal. Knapp, running in a zigzag fashion, reached the shed and stumbled through the open door, and in the same instant the men inside cut loose, sending Ed Dorsey out of his saddle in a hard, rolling fall.

Lowrie yelled—"Over here!"—and headed for the corrals. Tully's horse began to buck. He got the animal under control as Lowrie spilled out of his saddle and dived through the gate of the first corral. Then Tully was on the ground. He felt the numbing impact of a slug slamming against a rib on his right side; he fell flat on his face as another bullet dug into the dirt a foot from his head. He got his legs under him and lunged through the gate.

A bullet knocked splinters from a post above him, then Lowrie grabbed him and yanked him sideways. Tully went on over, the wind knocked out of him, and he heard Lowrie curse in a wild, crazy voice. Tully lay there behind the bottom log, his side aching with a dull, thumping pain.

"I thought for a minute we had 'em," Lowrie said bitterly. "We scared hell out of 'em and had 'em on the run. I threw three slugs at Knapp and missed every blamed one."

Smoke was rolling across the yard now, mostly from the barn. The house was a roaring inferno, flames breaking through the roof. The firing had stopped momentarily. Tully had his wind back, and now he felt the cold rage again that had been in him when he'd left Beth and walked with Lowrie to the stable. He had intended to bring Beth here as his wife, to live in this house where he had grown up, but now there was no house and in a few minutes there would be no barn.

Tully said: "I'm going after 'em."

"Don't be a fool," Lowrie snapped. "They're worse off than we are. That shed's no protection."

"I'm going after 'em," Tully said again. "Ed's out there in the yard. When the smoke clears, they'll plug him just to be sure they got him."

"Hang it," Lowrie shouted, "Dorsey's got nothing to live for! The way you kissed your girl, I thought you did."

Tully had his gun in his hand. It was not far to the corner of the barn, and by circling it he could come close to the shed. The smoke was thicker, billowing out across the yard in shifting clouds, almost hiding the shed and making accurate shooting difficult. He was unaware of the pain in his side; he could not let himself think of Beth and her words: *Whatever you do, Tully, come back.*

Ed Dorsey was lying out there, Ed Dorsey who had raised him and given him a home. Tully said—"Throw some lead, Lowrie."—and got to his feet.

"Stay here!" Lowrie bellowed. "That shed'll catch fire and they'll come out with their hands up. Stay here, I tell you."

But Tully couldn't stay. He plunged through the corral gate and ran to the barn; he heard Lowrie's shots as he emptied a six-gun, and he heard the answering shots from Knapp and his men. He reached the barn as a tongue of flame flicked out through a broken window; he went on around to the back. Inside, the fire was crackling like a thousand devils, then he cleared the far corner and saw that Lowrie was right about the shed. It was on fire, probably caught by sparks from the house.

For a moment Tully stood motionlessly, panting. As he waited, the shed door slammed open and Knapp and his men lunged out and headed for him, unaware that he was there. Lowrie was using his other gun now. One of the men spun and fell. Knapp and the other came on. There was little smoke here, the sunlight bright and sharp, and Knapp and the other man saw Tully just as they reached the barn.

Tully let go with his first shot. It was dead center, Knapp's hawk nose dissolving under the impact of the slug, killing him instantly. Tully threw another shot and missed. The Box K man had stopped, and, taking advantage of the brief moment he had when Tully got Knapp and missed a second shot, took his time before he squeezed trigger.

Tully went down, feeling as if he had been struck by an invisible club on his left shoulder, but he held onto his gun. The Box K man, overly confident now, ran toward him, firing as he came, wild shots that dug up the barnyard litter in front of Tully.

Lying flat on his belly, Tully tilted his gun up and drove two bullets into the man's middle. He sprawled headlong on the ground within ten feet of Tully and rolled over and lay still. Tully got to his hands and knees, then strength drained out of him and he toppled forward, and blackness swept in around him.

When Tully came to, he was lying in the bottom of a wagon, and Lowrie was saying: "I hope to heaven I can get him to the doc before this rattle trap rig falls apart."

Later he was aware of being carried into a house and up a flight of stairs. A crazy tag end of thought worried him. About Carradine. Stoking up a furnace. Being at the door. He tried to rise up and someone pushed him back, and Doc Wallace said: "I've got to probe for that slug." Then they had something under his nose and total blackness moved in around him once more.

He was still in bed when he came to, his shoulder a mass of bandages, and pain flowed through his body in a relentless current. But he was alive and he wanted to live. He shouted— "Beth!"—and was surprised that the sound that came out of his dry throat was only a whisper.

When he tried to sit up, he discovered he had no strength in him and cold sweat made a clammy film all over his body. He turned his head. A stand stood near his bed with some bottles and a pan on it. He managed to reach the pan and banged it against the side of the bed. Immediately he heard steps in the hall and Beth came in.

"Tully, you've got to be quiet."

She stood looking down at him, struggling with her lips to make them smile, and he managed a wink. He asked: "Ed?" She held her answer a moment. He said: "Don't lie. Ed's dead, ain't he?"

Beth nodded. "He lived a little while. He told Lowrie he wanted to be with Lon."

Tully closed his eyes. Maybe it was better this way. He hadn't supposed either one of the Dorseys had enough guts to fill a thimble, but he'd been wrong. He remembered how Ed had ridden up beside him, his gun talking, and he'd got Matt Quinn, the one really dangerous man in the Box K outfit. "I want to see Furnes," Tully said. "Then Bob."

She hesitated, not wanting to leave him, then she said: "You be quiet while I'm gone." She left the room.

It seemed to him she was gone for a long time. He figured out exactly what he'd say, lying here with his eyes closed. He was in Carradine's house, he supposed. No, Beth's house now, and maybe it always had been. There was a lot about Carradine they'd never know, for now it was impossible to distinguish between the truth and the lies in what he'd said.

Furnes came in presently, Doc Wallace behind him, and then Mulcahy. Tully said: "I told Beth. . . ."

"We figured we'd tag along just to hear you talk," Wallace said. "You were up there, shaking hands with Saint Peter, you know, and I don't figure on you finishing the handshaking if I can help it."

"All right," Tully said. "You're a devil of an outfit. . . ." Then he stopped, remembering what Lowrie had said about some men who could fight and some who couldn't and that was the way of it. Anyhow, it wasn't what he'd planned to say. "About Lowrie . . . ?"

"I was wrong," Wallace said bluntly. "I've apologized to him."

"Takes more'n that," Tully said. "You're gonna start being friends. Visit him. All of you. Get Svenson and O'Brien and the rest of the valley out there to Anchor 9."

"I'll take care of it," Mulcahy said. "I'm to blame. I should have seen how it was."

"Lowrie's to blame as much as anybody," Furnes said stubbornly, "being a pretty cold fish, but we'll make it different."

They went out, and a moment later Bob Hoven came in. He looked old as Lowrie had said he was, old and uncertain of himself. He said: "You sure did a job, Tully. I knew. . . ."

"Maybe you knew more'n I did," Tully said, "but what I wanted to say was that I'm beholden to you for sending for me and saving my hide that night in the Casino. Took a lot of guts. I've been thinking about this star, too. Kind of like wearing it. Soon as I get on my feet, I'll take your office over if you want to go to work somewhere. I don't figure it'll be a full-time job now."

Hoven straightened as if twenty years had rolled off his back. "I'd sure like it if you would. Furnes told me I could go to work for him."

Wheeling, Hoven left the room, unable to say any more. A sense of well-being filled Tully.

Beth hustled in, saying: "Your room's the busiest place in Starbuck, but now the visiting's over."

"Not quite." He took Beth's hand as she sat down on the edge of the bed. "Lowrie told you about finding the judge?"

She nodded. "He told me."

"The judge wanted me to tell you he loved you. I don't reckon a dying man would lie."

"I'm sure he didn't," she said quietly. "I want to remember the good things he did and in time maybe I can forget the others."

"I'm a good fixer," he said.

"You're more than that," she said softly. "You're the bravest man I know."

"I'll tell you the truth. I was so. . . ." He stopped. Let her think what she wanted to. Maybe someday they'd be spinning campfire yarns about him the way they did about his father. And maybe his and Beth's kids would say—"Tully Bain? Why, he was my dad."—proud-like, the way he had thought about Red Bain.

"I'm going down and fix you some broth." She bent over and kissed him. "Now will you be quiet?"

"I ain't going nowhere," he said. "Not today."

ABOUT THE AUTHOR

Wayne D. Overholser won three Spur Awards from the Western Writers of America and has a long list of fine Western titles to his credit. He was born in Pomeroy, Washington, and attended the University of Montana, University of Oregon, and the University of Southern California before becoming a public schoolteacher and principal in various Oregon communities. He began writing for Western pulp magazines in 1936 and within a couple of years was a regular contributor to Street & Smith's *Western Story Magazine* and Fiction House's *Lariat Story Magazine*. *Buckaroo's Code* (1947) was his first Western novel and remains one of his best. In the 1950s and 1960s, having retired from academic work to concentrate on writing, he would publish as many as four books a year under his own name or a pseudonym, most prominently as Joseph Wayne. *The Violent Land* (1954), *The Lone Deputy* (1957), *The Bitter Night* (1961), and *Riders of the Sundowns* (1997) are among the finest of the Overholser titles. *The Sweet and Bitter Land* (1950), *Bunch Grass* (1955), and *Land of Promises* (1962) are among the best Joseph Wayne titles, and *Law Man* (1953) is a most rewarding novel under the Lee Leighton pseudonym. Overholser's Western novels, whatever the byline, are based on a solid knowledge of the history and customs of the 19th-Century West, particularly when set in his two favorite Western states, Oregon and Colorado. Many of his novels are first-person narratives, a technique that tends to bring an added dimension of vividness to the frontier experiences of his narrators and frequently, as in *Cast a Long Shadow* (1957), the female characters one encounters are among the most memorable. He wrote his numerous novels with a consistent skill and an uncommon sensitivity to the depths of human character. Almost invariably, his stories weave a spell of their own with their scenes and images of social and economic forces often in conflict and the diverse ways of life and personalities that made the American Western frontier so unique a time and place in human history.